TEMPERED STEEL

JANET MCNULTY

This is a work of fiction. Names, characters, places, and incidents within are the product of the author's imagination or are used fictitiously, and any resemblance to actual persons, living or dead, business establishments, events, or location is entirely coincidental. The publisher does not have any control over and does not assume any responsibility for author or third-party websites or their content.

Tempered Steel

ISBN-10: 0615773338 (MMP Publishing)
ISBN-13: 978-0615773339

Printed in the United States of America

If you purchase this book without a cover, you should be aware that this book is stolen property. It was reported as "unsold and destroyed" to the publisher, and neither the author nor the publisher has received any payment for this "stripped book".

For any who have ever had to face adversity.

Praise for *Dystopia:*

"Fast-paced and well-crafted, I can't wait for the next installment!"

"If you like a fast moving story with a David against Goliath theme, you'll enjoy Dystopia."

"I wish there are better words to describe how much I love this book. It's AWESOME. I love how the storyline glides from the starting to the end and the way the author describes the characters and the settings of the book…The ending was PURE SUSPENSE!"

TEMPERED STEEL

CHAPTER

ONE

Officer Burroughs mercilessly eyed the men lined outside against the wall in the center of the Waste Management Plant. A riot broke out at the plant soon after the video aired over all of television showing Dana's interrogation by Colonel Fernau. Men had attacked the officers, men who were angry, desperate, and seeking vengeance. Some fires still burned. Bodies still littered the area, waiting to be dumped in the incinerator.

Officer Burroughs didn't care if those waiting for execution instigated the riot or not. He just wanted to make an example. Determined to demonstrate his authority, he had 20 men randomly rounded up.

Officer Burroughs raised his arm as his officers aimed their guns at those sentenced to death. His narrowed eyes focused on each of them. A baritone voice broke the silence.

Pausing, Officer Burroughs searched for its source. It came from one of the condemned. He lowered his arm slightly.

> Take up the torch.
> Lift it high.
> Let fear be scorched.
> Let Tyranny die.

Officer Burroughs couldn't believe his ears. The man sang the old song from the foolish rebellion of 125 years ago. A group of people had decided that the individual was better than the collective society. Government forces cut them down easily and destroyed any memory of it.

"Idiots," muttered Officer Burroughs. He would enjoy killing them.

His eyes locked with Mad Dog's. A pleased smile crept across his face. *Lock me in the freezer, will you?* Officer Burroughs raised his arm again and dropped it.

"Fire!"

Gunfire echoed around the area as the officers released their terror. The men lined before them dropped to the ground. Pooling blood puddled into a small pond under the bodies.

Satisfied, Officer Burroughs turned around to head back to his office. Colonel Fernau stood behind him. The colonel's menacing look chilled Officer Burroughs to the core. Something was terribly wrong.

"A word with you," said Colonel Fernau, his nose now crooked from where Dana had punched him.

"Why, yes," said Officer Burroughs, trepidation in his voice. "This way."

Officer Burroughs led Colonel Fernau through the plant and up the stairs to his office. He noticed an unusual number of armed guards, officers whose faces he did not recognize. Sweat formed at the base of his neck.

"After you," said Colonel Fernau as Officer Burroughs opened the door to his office.

Once inside, the colonel shut the door, making certain the latch clicked.

"Is there something I can do for you, colonel?" asked Officer Burroughs as he moved behind the desk.

Colonel Fernau paced the room. "I understand that there was a riot yesterday."

"Yes, there was," said Officer Burroughs, unsure of where the conversation went.

"And you handled it of course."

"The instigators were executed this morning, as you well saw."

"So I did."

Officer Burroughs noted the way the colonel held his stick. "Why all of the extra security?"

"Just a precaution," Colonel Fernau waved away the question.

"Is there anything else?" Officer Burroughs asked, tentatively.

Colonel Fernau stopped directly in front of Officer Burroughs, staring him right in the eyes. "As I understand it, you were locked in the kitchen freezer for most of last night."

"Yes."

"How did that happen?"

"A new worker, Mad Dog, thought it would be funny. He was among those executed."

"So he was," said Colonel Fernau, "And how did he lock you in there?"

"He and his friends caught me off-guard," answered Officer Burroughs, more sweat forming on his neck.

"Caught you off-guard?" Colonel Fernau's eyes burned into Officer Burroughs. "And I suppose the riot caught you off-guard as well."

Officer Burroughs tugged at his collar. "Yes, it did."

"You're sweating, Officer Burroughs. Is there something wrong?"

"No."

"You seem nervous."

"Do I?" Immediately, Officer Burroughs bit his tongue, wishing he hadn't said that.

"Are you aware that Dana Ginary has escaped?"

"No."

Colonel Fernau arched an eyebrow. "But you are, undoubtedly, aware of the video that aired last evening. The one that sheds unfortunate light upon our president and first councilman of the eastern region."

"How could I not? It aired on every television within Dystopia."

"So it did." Colonel Fernau picked an object up from the desk and examined it. He let it drop to the floor and shatter. "Interesting thing about that broadcast."

"Interesting, sir?" Worry filled Officer Burroughs.

"Yes," said Colonel Fernau, "it came from your computer terminal."

This news shocked Officer Burroughs. He hadn't been on his computer since yesterday morning. "It couldn't…"

"The signal has been traced to here."

"But, colonel, I'd never… I didn't…"

"Who else has access to this office?"

"No one," said Officer Burroughs.

"And you have the only key?"

"Yes, but…"

"Officer Burroughs, I suggest you quit playing games with me."

"I didn't…"

"Then how do you explain your computer being used to hack the media network and broadcast a video that started riots in both the eastern and western regions?"

"I can't. A hacker maybe?"

"Our encryption codes are nearly impossible to break. It would take a hacker days to wade through them."

"But…"

"Frankly, Officer Burroughs, I don't care if your office was broken into and your computer was hacked. You disgust me. An ant has more value than you.

"First Councilman Michaels wants the situation contained, and the riot yesterday clearly indicates that you are incapable of handling this place. You're a disgrace to Dystopia."

Before Officer Burroughs could say anything, Colonel Fernau whacked him with his stick. He leered over the man with a sneer. Officer Burroughs looked at him through a bloody eye.

"I will get to the bottom of this," snarled Colonel Fernau, "and you and I are going to get to know each other very well."

Colonel Fernau walked to the door and opened it. "Take him away."

Officers rushed into the room, placing a bag over Officer Burroughs' head. Without incident, they dragged him away.

Colonel Fernau noticed a box tucked away in the office. Using his stick, he lifted one of the flaps, revealing a platter of cookies and pastries. "Such weakness."

He marched out of the room, boots clicking on the bare floor.

CHAPTER
TWO

The train bounced and jerked as it rolled down the tracks. Dana lay crumpled on the floor amidst bits of hay and dirt. She had cried herself to sleep after George's death. Images of it played and replayed in her mind. The locket remained clutched tightly in her hand.

Slowly, Dana awoke. She rubbed her eyes and tear-stained face. Sitting up, she peered at the locket. Dana opened it. Inside rested the picture of a woman she had never met, but felt she had known. The woman had strawberry blonde hair and hazel eyes, staring at her with a mixture of sorrow and joy. This was George's wife.

She's beautiful, thought Dana.

She snapped the locket shut and put it around her neck with the computer disk that Sanders had given her, the only remnants of her life in Dystopia. Dana looked out at the barren landscape that whizzed by. She had never been this far beyond the wall. Not knowing how long she had been on the train, Dana decided now was as good a time as any to hop off. She knew that if she remained too long, she would eventually reach the western region of Dystopia. *And be arrested, no doubt.*

She scooted over to the open car door. Peering out, Dana gauged the train's speed. The train slowed down some. *Must be a switch up ahead.* She was familiar enough with trains to know that switches lined the tracks. Each time a train neared one, it had to slow down or risk derailing. The only exceptions were the rails that were built specifically for the high-speed passenger trains.

The squalling wheels told her that it was now or never. Bracing herself for the possibility of death, or worse, Dana leapt from the train car. Weightlessness held her a moment before she crashed into the sandy earth. Tumbling and rolling, the world seemed a blur until she stopped.

Once stilled, Dana lay on the ground as the train continued onward. Her left shoulder throbbed. Knowing she had dislocated it, Dana popped it back in place. Sharp pain seized her body, forcing her to remain slumped over for several minutes. Once it had subsided enough, she stood up and examined her new surroundings while slowly moving her shoulder.

Eternal sand stretched before her. Tiny, green plants that barely stuck out of the ground formed what looked like black specks. Puffs of sand drifted over her feet. Dana noticed a sand devil in the distance as the wind picked up and then died.

She bent down and scooped some of the grit into her

hands, allowing it to fall between her fingers. *It really is a barren wasteland.* Dana remembered the stories she had been told. She had never believed them until now.

Spotting a tower up ahead, Dana walked toward it, hoping that it meant there were people nearby. She walked slowly, surprised at how warm the afternoon sun felt. Back home, the cold season had started. Dana figured things were different here.

Pools of water appeared before her. Desperate for a drink, Dana ran to the first few before she realized they were mirages. Cursing, she wished she would find real sources of water. Her parched throat ached.

After hours of walking, Dana was no nearer to the tower. "How far is it?" she demanded of the environment around her.

The only reply she received was a couple of whirling dust devils.

Her feet plopped on the ground with harsh thuds. Starting to feel dehydrated, Dana staggered around, trying to keep the tower in view. The sun had dipped low in the sky. Feeling defeated, she sank to the ground as the sky grew increasingly dark.

If Dana thought that the days in the wasteland were too warm, its nights were frigid cold. Exposed, she hugged her knees close to her as she shivered. Dana looked around, but didn't find anything in the darkness that resembled shelter.

A howl sounded in the distance. Frightened, Dana's senses jolted to heightened alert. She scanned the expanse, but the moonless night concealed everything. Another howl sounded. Dana remembered her grandfather telling her stories about wild dogs roaming the wasteland. She hoped she wasn't on the menu.

Another howl sounded. This time it was close.

Her pulse racing, Dana whipped her head around, searching for the source. She heard a growl nearby. Another sounded. Before Dana knew it, two coyotes attacked each other, snarling and growling as they fought. The sounds echoed across the expanse, filling Dana with fear.

Then, it stopped.

Glowing eyes appeared in the night. They watched Dana as they inched closer. Not knowing what to do, Dana snatched a rock and chucked it at them. It thumped on the ground and disappeared. Immediately, she wished she hadn't done that.

She watched in terror as the glowing eyes approached, becoming attached to hungry coyotes that thought she made a perfect meal. Dana backed up some. The snarling behind her told her that she was completely surrounded. Panic stricken, Dana got on all fours, not knowing what to do.

Everything went still.

The coyotes pointed their noses in the air, and after sniffing it, they darted away into the night, leaving Dana alone. Relieved, she relaxed a little. *Why did they leave?* In answer to her thought, a soft roar started up behind her. It grew louder as it neared. Before Dana had time to realize what happened, the wind whipped around her, blowing sand everywhere. The grit pelted her exposed skin, delivering sharp stings.

Confused, Dana squirmed around, trying to escape, but her efforts proved useless. After being pounded by the sand, she tore off her shirt and wrapped it around her head to protect her face. She hunkered down, putting her face into her arms. Though she managed to protect it, the rest of her remained exposed.

Her ears ached from the roaring wind. Grit filled her mouth. Choking, Dana tried to spit it out as it absorbed what saliva she had. The onslaught raged around her. As Dana started to think it would never end, it stopped. As the roar subsided and the pelting sand ceased, Dana unwrapped her head. Half buried, she looked around. The landscape had changed.

"Maybe I should have stayed home," she said to the world, thinking that she had jumped off the train and into Hell.

Dana wrapped her shirt around herself and stretched out. If she died before morning, so be it.

CHAPTER

THREE

Officer Burroughs lay on the cold, concrete floor in a pool of his own blood. He watched Colonel Fernau's shiny, black boots pace around him. "Why are you doing this?" he asked. "I have always been a loyal party member."

"It is of little consequence," said Colonel Fernau. "You have become expendable."

"But I don't know anything."

"We shall see."

"I have rights."

"You have been branded a terrorist. You're rights are what I say they are. And I say that you have none."

Colonel Fernau struck Officer Burroughs again. The man grunted each time the switch hit him.

Officer Burroughs coughed as he choked on his blood-filled spit. "I swear I know nothing."

"So you keep claiming."

"I don't!"

Colonel Fernau kneeled beside Officer Burroughs, using his gloved hand to wipe the dribble from the man's face. He picked up an electric baton. Maliciously, he rammed it into Officer Burroughs' upturned side, reveling in the way the electricity caused the man to flop about like a dead fish.

Pain coursed through Officer Burroughs, his teeth chattering from the shock that surged through him. Blood and spit escaped his parted lips flying everywhere. "I... don't..."

"Tell me!"

Colonel Fernau rammed the electric baton into Officer Burroughs again. Screams of agonizing pain bounced off the concrete walls of the interrogation room. Music to Colonel Fernau's ears. He dug the baton deeper until the smell of burning flesh filled his nostrils.

"How many members of the resistance are in Waste Management?"

"I don't have an exact number."

"Pity."

Colonel Fernau picked up Officer Burroughs and threw him across the room. A sickening crunch emanated from the man. Moaning, Officer Burroughs vainly tried to crawl across the concrete floor. Colonel Fernau straightened his pristine uniform. He casually walked over to his prey, his boots clacking against the hard surface with impending doom. With immense pressure, he dug the sharp heel of his boot on Officer Burroughs' outstretched hand, digging into the flesh until blood oozed.

The door opened, and men marched in with a table,

chairs, and a bunch of thin, long sticks. Officer Burroughs felt himself lifted off the floor and plopped into one of the metal chairs in front of the table.

"Know what this is?" asked Colonel Fernau as he waved one of the sticks in front of Officer Burroughs' face. "In another part of the world, interrogators would insert one of these under the fingernails and light it. Then, as it slowly burned, they would wait for the person to talk or allow their fingers to be burned off."

The officers seized Officer Burroughs' hands and slammed them on the table. He struggled, but was too dazed to be a match for them. Colonel Fernau slowly approached. He took one of the sticks and inserted it under one of the nails. Sharp pain gripped Officer Burroughs.

"Whenever you wish to talk," Colonel Fernau lit the slit of wood.

Squirming, Officer Burroughs watched in horror as the small flame burned, drawing closer. Slowly, it traveled down the slender stick, the heat intensifying.

"I don't know anything."

"Then I shall watch you suffer."

Searing heat attacked Officer Burroughs' fingers, forcing him to howl in pain. "Please, I know nothing."

Colonel Fernau's sadistic, icy stare showed that he didn't care.

More agonizing pain gripped Officer Burroughs' fingers. Desperately, he tried to pull the sticks out, but strong hands held him down.

"I grow tired of this," Colonel Fernau said.

He stepped to the door of the interrogation room and yanked it open. "Get this filth out of here."

Officers hauled Officer Burroughs to his feet. They dragged him out of the room.

"Take him back to the Waste Management plant," ordered Colonel Fernau, "and see to it that he suffers an unfortunate accident."

Officer Burroughs may not have aired that video, but someone did. Colonel Fernau was determined to find out who had.

CHAPTER
FOUR

The morning sun shone through the slits in Dana's eyes, forcing her to open them. Groaning, she sat up. Her throat ached for a drop of water, and her stomach refused to be silent. Feeling lightheaded, she stared out at the vacant expanse. The tower loomed ahead of her, taunting her. Dana rose to her feet and continued on.

Like before, the hours passed faster than she could walk. Her movements were sloppy as she staggered about, trying to keep the tower ahead of her. Weaving to the left, Dana steered herself back. After a few more moments, she veered to the right as her sense of balance faded. Stopping, Dana looked for the tower, found it, and continued on. She knew eventually that she would reach it, though she began to think that she would die beforehand.

Live for the both of us.

"George?"

Dana whirled around, convinced that she had heard George's voice. Only empty space greeted her. Disheartened, Dana realized that she was beginning to hallucinate. She licked her dry, cracked lips to moisten them. It only made them burn all the more.

Her skin itched. Dana scratched it. Instantly, a burning sensation covered her arm from her irritating the sunburn she had received from her hours of wandering in its harsh rays. Scolding herself, Dana resisted the urge to scratch it even more.

Her breaths came in ragged gasps. Exhausted, she flopped to the sandy ground. She hadn't eaten or drunk anything since the morning of the break-in to the media center. She wished she were back there. George would still be alive.

Guilt panged Dana. *His death is my fault.* She shook her head, dismissing such thoughts from her mind. *It won't help me now.*

The chirping of a bird caught her attention. In the two days she had roamed the desert, Dana had not seen any signs of life, except for the coyotes that had tried to make supper out of her. She looked up at the bird. It chirped again. Dana suddenly realized where it had perched itself. The tower, she thought. She had finally reached it.

With renewed strength, Dana ran down the sandy hill to the tower. Her rubbery legs barely carried her. Tripping, Dana rolled down the hill, getting dirt in crevices she didn't want to think about. She righted herself and ran to her destination.

Dana stopped. Glancing around, her heart sank as she realized that no signs of people were to be found. The humming of the tower mocked her. Frustrated, she kicked its metal base. Sinking into the sand once again, Dana screamed and yelled at the cruelty that the desert had dealt her.

Plunk!

Dana looked up. She thought she had heard something.

Plunk!

She did hear something. Excitement coursed through her as she jumped to her feet and searched for the source of the sound. Rummaging through the sand, Dana found a faucet.

Plunk!

Small drops of water escaped it as they fell into a small hole in the sand. Thinking of only quenching her thirst, Dana rushed to the faucet and pumped the handle. Only gurgling air came through. She pumped the handle again. Nothing. Though water dripped from the faucet head, she couldn't get it to come out in a stream.

Desperate, Dana cupped her hands underneath the faucet, allowing the drops to fill them. She guzzled it when enough had pooled. She shoved her hands under the faucet again.

Once she had soothed her throat, Dana stood up and looked around. The humming of the tower and wires told her that it worked. That meant people had to come there to maintain it. Dana inspected the lines that ran down the length of the desert.

"These go somewhere," she said to herself.

Knowing she could not remain where she was, Dana followed the power line, hoping that it would lead her to some sort of settlement.

~ ~ ~

Everyone gathered in the dimly lit room, their sullen faces trying not to glance at one another. Simon took note of who had made it and who hadn't. The absence of George and Dana filled his heart with sorrow. Somehow, he always knew they wouldn't make it.

"Anyone else?" asked Charles.

"No," said Amy. "The ones here are the only ones who survived."

"We can recruit new members," said Simon.

"George isn't here," said Charles.

"I'm aware of that," replied Simon.

"That Ginary girl probably got him killed," grumbled Charles. He closed his mouth when he received a scolding look from Simon. "I'm just saying…"

"I know what you are saying," said Simon, "but it's not necessary. George knew the risks. He made his choice."

"But he's dead," said Amy.

"I know," replied Simon, "and we mourn his loss. I wonder if she survived."

Charles began to open his mouth, but stopped. Simon was in no mood for his complaints.

"What do we do now?" asked another in the room.

Simon looked at the television in the corner of the room. President Klens' face filled the screen as she rambled on about the dangers of independent people. Halloway's face appeared suddenly, along with a picture of Dana. Simon turned up the volume.

"Dana Ginary is believed to be a dangerous person associated with the resistance, a group of terrorists bent on disrupting our ordered life. Last evening, she gave a speech filled with hate and lies at a ceremony meant to honor her.

Apparently, she used the trusting members of the Detention Center to free known extremists. If you have any information, you are urged to call this number."

Simon clicked off the television, thoughts percolating through his mind. He got an idea. If the government insisted on branding Dana as a traitor, they should brand her as a hero. Her face was known, and her words did spark a few riots across the country.

"I think we can make good use of this," said Simon.

"Pardon?" asked the others in the room.

"President Klens has decided to smear Dana's name, but we can tell the truth."

"What are you proposing?" asked Amy.

"Dana's speech did cause waves in certain sectors," said Simon. "What if we use her face as the face of the resistance? People will recognize her. We can tell the truth of how she was used by our government. We can use her to promote our cause."

"Wouldn't that in effect make us just as bad as those who coerced her in the first place?" asked Amy.

Simon's face fell. Unfortunately, Amy's statement had an element of truth. "What do you suggest?"

"We just tell the truth about how the government used her and then dumped her," said Amy. "We can use elements of her speech the other night to highlight what she believes in. As for spreading our message, I think we should find other means."

"Very well," said Simon.

"I also think we should be on the lookout for her. She might still be alive. We are her only friends now," said Amy.

"Charles?" asked Simon, noting the look on his friend's face.

"You know how I feel about her," mumbled Charles, "but I guess we can't let them get their hands on her."

"Then it's settled," said Simon. "Get a video made telling Dana's story to counteract the state propaganda. Tell everyone to be on the lookout for Dana. If they find her, they are to bring her here."

The meeting ended and the room bustled to life as people left to carry out their tasks. Simon hoped Dana still lived. He hoped that Colonel Fernau had not captured her.

CHAPTER

FIVE

Exhausted, Dana walked into an abandoned city. Its ruins surrounded her as she strolled along the cracked pavement. Her foot hit something metallic. Carefully, Dana picked up a rusted sign with one word on it: Omaha. She dropped it. The name was unfamiliar to her.

Her shoes crunched on pieces of the crumbling asphalt as Dana continued into the city among skeletons of once magnificent buildings. It seemed like a perfect haven for ghosts.

She stopped. A bobcat darted across the road. Chiding herself for being easily startled, Dana continued. The deafening silence wore on her. *Still no people.*

Crash!

Dana whirled around. A steel girder had finally collapsed under the weight of the building it had been a part of. Calming her nerves, Dana continued onward.

The wind picked up. Shivering, Dana watched as trails of sand snaked across the ground, guiding the path of a tumbleweed. She felt isolated, alone. With only the wind for comfort, Dana wandered the maze of streets as she explored the ruined city.

"This must have been a lively place at some point," she said to herself. "I wonder what happened."

She came upon a vehicle stripped of its paint and tires. The windshield had been smashed long ago. The find excited Dana. It meant that when people had once lived in this place, they couldn't have been much different from her.

Not liking the silence, Dana decided to sing a song that she had heard once as a child. She did not understand the meaning behind the words, but she knew that they were important, as though they described a time when destruction reigned over hope.

As Dana sang the song, memories flooded her mind of the time when she first heard it. Before her sixth birthday, many had gathered to peacefully protest new regulations concerning their ability to heat their homes in the winter and cool them in the summer. The new regulations restricted energy usage for each individual, all in the name of preserving the planet and precious resources. Many froze in the winter or roasted in the summer even before the new rules. Only those with connections escaped the rationing.

Others who joined the protest wanted the right to elect their own leaders, stating that it was wrong that President Klens and First Councilman Seth Michaels inherited their positions of power. They wanted to determine their own fate.

Dana's grandfather had joined the protest, stating that "man was never meant to be ruled."

Dana had been forbidden to go, but had snuck out of the house anyway. Her first regret in life. She wandered to the square where the protest had taken place. Many just held signs, stating their right to determine how much heat their homes had, how much they ate, or where they worked.

Then, the marching boots came. Dana remembered watching as armed officers stormed the gathered crowd. Without warning, they opened fire with machine guns. She watched in fear as people dropped to the ground, never to get up again.

Dana remembered screaming as she hunkered behind lifeless bodies, covering her ears. Somehow, her grandfather had found her. He scooped her into his arms and tied his scarf around her eyes to block the horrible scene. But the scarf didn't hide it all.

Weeks passed before she was able to sleep without being held by either her parents or grandfather. Dana pushed the memories from her mind as she sang the song that the protesters had sung that fateful day. It dated back to a time before Dystopia existed, but its true origins were unknown.

Fires burning,
children weeping,
the Lady stands alone.

Riots raging,
people yelling,
why this madness come?

Janet McNulty

Gunfire exploding,
women screaming,
tears escape her eyes.
Soldiers marching,
people running,
the Lady watches all.

Above them towering,
her torch shining,
she's forgotten in her harbor.

Freedom dying,
darkness falling,
she mourns the loss of her friend.

"Have I not," she asks,
"stood here proudly?
Why do you ignore me?"

Now she's crumbling,
her torch fading,
still for us she stands.

One girl searching,
she is treading,
upon the Lady's bed.

A rare finding,
forgotten and lying,
the Lady's torch is unearthed.

The girl's arm lifting,
torch light blazing,
the Lady sees and smiles.
"At last you remember me.
Take my fiery light.
Carry it with you always.

Take up the torch.
Lift it high.
Let fear be scorched.
Let tyranny die."

Her voice echoed across the area, bouncing off the buildings. Still no sign of life. Darkness settled around her. Not wanting to spend another night exposed, she approached a small building, its door hanging precariously from its hinges. Cautiously, Dana stepped inside.

"Hello," she called.

No answer. She didn't think she would get one, but decided to try anyway. Dana walked through the small interior over rusted aluminum cans. She found a small corner and curled up there, eventually falling asleep.

"Nothing," said a harsh voice. "Pickings keep getting less and less."

Dana bolted upright and carefully peeked out around the door. Four men stood yards away from her. Filthy, tattered rags covered their bodies. Dana smelled their stench. They hadn't bathed in weeks. She wondered if they even knew what a bar of soap was for.

"I'm telling you we need to go somewhere else," said a second man.

"No," raged the first.

"There isn't anything here. Even the people we garner our things from have stopped traveling this area," continued the second.

A part of Dana was overjoyed at seeing people. She started to go to them, but stopped. Their mannerisms seemed odd. She decided to exercise caution. Taking a step back inside, her foot crunched a can on the floor, sending it flying across the room. Cringing, Dana remained, still hoping they hadn't heard.

"What was that?" The men turned in her direction.

Fearful, Dana bolted through the door and into the streets away from the four men.

"Get her!"

She heard feet pounding the crumbling pavement behind her. Though tired and weak, Dana found the strength necessary to run. Her breathing grew harsh as she fled.

One of them men jumped in front of her. "Boo!"

Dana skidded to a halt and turned. She continued down a path she didn't know. Still, the men pursued her.

Another popped up before her. "Where are you going, sweetheart?"

Frightened, Dana turned in another direction. *They're everywhere!* Panting, she continued racing through the unfamiliar territory. Her foot struck something. Hopping, Dana regained her balance and kept going.

She veered to the left. One of the men waited for her. Startled, Dana turned around to find the others. She had been surrounded. Her eyes darting from each of them, she looked all around for a way to escape.

Dana tried to dart between them. Instantly, strong hands snatched her, pulling her off her feet.

"Let me go!" screamed Dana as she struggled. She kneed one of them in the groin. In response, he brought his fist to her face, causing another large welt to form.

"Hey, sweetheart," said one. "What's the hurry?" His ragged clothing hung from his scarecrow-like body.

"Yeah, we only want to get to know you."

Dana detested the way he said that.

"Let me go!"

"Now hold on there," said the man who was clearly in charge. "Who are you and how did you get here?" His six-foot stature towered over the others. Blackened teeth filled his mouth.

Dana looked at him, trying to discern if his intentions were honest. In the back of her mind, she knew she was in serious trouble. "Dana."

"What brought you here?"

"My feet."

"Don't get cute with me."

"I jumped off a train and have been wandering since," said Dana, knowing there was little use in lying.

"Hopped off a train?" said one, tugging on the greasy strings that made up his hair.

The leader silenced him. He examined her clothing and a wicked smile appeared on his face. "What we have here is a runaway. Another one of those people from that country. So you thought you could make it out here, eh?"

Dana kept her mouth shut.

"We've run into many of your kind," continued the man, "Most of them die out here. Seems like you'll do the same."

"Let me go!" Dana struggled some more.

"You think you can make it out there alone?" scoffed the man.

Dana preferred to take her chances rather than remain with them. She did not like the way they looked at her.

"We should take her with us," said a small, swarthy man, "and have a little fun."

"I saw her first," protested another. "She's mine."

"Oh, yeah?"

"Enough!" yelled the leader. "She's coming with us." The man stroked Dana's hair. "Perhaps she can provide us with a little entertainment before we carve her up."

Immediately, a gag torn from the leader's jacket was shoved into her mouth as her hands were tied. Dana tried to resist, but was no match for them.

"Let's get out of here."

The men left the ruined city, taking Dana with them.

CHAPTER

SIX

"I want her found!" President Klens' voice bellowed from the view screen on the wall.

"She will be," said Seth Michaels.

Kenny remained on the balcony, listening to the exchange. The anger in the president's voice was very evident. His father's mood had been dismal the past week, ever since Dana had escaped.

Did you know I was to be killed as well?

Dana's questions plagued his mind. What did she mean, he thought. His father had promised him that she would be allowed her choice of career if she helped them. Why would she accuse him of lying to her?

"Will be?" screeched President Klens' voice.

"She escaped to the wastelands," said Seth Michaels.

"What?"

Kenny cringed at her shrill voice.

"How did she get there?" demanded President Klens.

Seth Michaels chewed his tongue a moment. "She managed to board a freight train bound for the western region. We checked when it arrived there, but she was not aboard. I believe she jumped off somewhere in between."

"Really? And what alerted you to that possibility?" President Klens' sarcasm did not go unnoticed.

"Madam President," said Seth Michaels, "she is as good as dead out there. Nothing lives in that barren expanse except bandits and thieves. If the elements do not kill her, they will."

This seemed to appease the president for the moment. "I want her face on every broadcast. Instill in the people's minds the danger that she is. Within the next few weeks, everyone should be talking about how Dana Ginary is a threat to our society and way of life."

"But if she is dead…" began Seth Michaels.

"And what if she isn't? What if by some chance she manages to crawl out of the desert and back into Dystopia? I'll not risk her starting a rebellion. I'll not risk her becoming a hero. I want her reputation destroyed, so that if she does show up again, the people will willingly hand her over. This is your mess, First Councilman. Clean it up!"

"Yes, ma'am," relented Seth Michaels. "It will be done as you have asked."

He clicked a button and the screen turned off.

"Kenny?"

Kenny left the balcony and entered the room his father occupied.

"Where would Dana go? Do you know?"

Kenny shook his head. "No, father."

"You were her friend while in the same class."

"Yes, but she and I were always of two different mind-sets," said Kenny.

"So you told me." Seth Michaels paced the room, trying to determine what to do next.

"Will that be all, father?"

"Yes." Seth Michaels waved his son away. He paused before a photo of Dana. "Dana Ginary, where are you?"

~ ~ ~

Dana tripped as the rope leashing her to her captors pulled taut. She regained her balance. Weak and slightly dizzy, Dana feared that she might die in the company of these bandits. Not a prospect she desired.

"Come on, you lazy squaw." One of the men yanked on the rope, nearly knocking her off her feet.

Dana had no idea what the word squaw was supposed to mean. It was one of those banned words in Dystopia, deemed as hate speech.

"Come on," hissed the man with the rope as she lagged behind again.

She picked up the pace, her legs refusing to work. Dana glanced at the leader and the disk and George's locket that hung on his belt. He had taken them from her earlier. Silently, Dana vowed to get them back.

"This looks like a good place to stop," said the leader. "We should be back by tomorrow."

The man with the rope dragged Dana to a half dead tree,

forcing her to sit down. He tied the other end of the rope to his ankle to make it more difficult for her to escape.

The leader tossed a bag at her. "Fix us something to eat."

Dana glared at him. Not knowing how to make a fire, she gathered some wood together and then stared at it.

"What are you, incompetent?"

One of the others pushed her out of the way. He snatched a couple of rocks and clacked them together, producing sparks. Once the wood caught fire, he tossed the rocks at her.

"That's how you do it. Now get something cooking before we decide you are useless."

Wishing she could bash his face in, Dana yanked the bag. She opened the flap and looked inside. Something attracted her attention. Carefully, Dana pulled out a bunch of dried belladonna. Having been taught about herbs and their uses by her mother, Dana knew exactly what to do with it.

She spotted their jug of alcohol. While the men busied themselves with plans about her future, Dana snatched the jug. She popped the cork. Crumbling the belladonna in her hands, Dana carefully put it in the jug. She swished it some to mix it in, hoping it would dissolve before they drank from it.

"Hey!" The leader marched up to her and grabbed the jug from her. "What are you doing with this?"

"Using it to flavor your supper," said Dana.

The leader pulled out the cork. His nostrils flared as he sniffed it. "Keep your hands off this in the future."

He walked away, joining his friends. Together, they laughed, taking giant swigs from the jug as they passed it around.

"Hurry up with our supper!"

Dana searched the bag again for anything that could be made into a meal. She found some dead lizards. Forcing herself not to gag, Dana skinned them and placed them over the fire. She had never cooked outside of a kitchen before and was unsure of what to do.

When they seemed done enough, and not too badly burned, she placed them on some cloth she found in the bag and brought them over to the men.

"Took you long enough," said one.

"What is this?" asked the leader.

"Supper," said Dana, holding the cooked lizards out to him.

"Not much of a cook, are you?"

"No," came Dana's curt reply.

"Well, at least there are other ways you can serve us."

Dana did not like the way his eyes traveled the length of her body. He licked his lips while greedily looking at her. She tossed the lizards in his lap and marched away.

"Thank you, sweetheart."

Secluded in her corner, Dana watched as her captors ate and drank. She hoped the belladonna would take effect soon. *Did I use enough?* She worked the rope around her wrists loose. Though they had left it loose enough for her to work, it was still tight.

More laughter escaped from them as they feasted and emptied their jug. Dana's head popped up. The thought that she might have guessed wrong entered her mind. She continued working the rope loose from around her wrists while pleading that her plan succeeded.

The men's speech slurred. She watched intently as one

by one, they dropped off. Dana ripped the rope from around her wrists. Finally freed, she hopped over to the leader. Swiftly, Dana searched him for the locket and disk.

Her fingers touched them. Thrilled, Dana ripped them from his belt and put them around her neck. A hand seized her wrist. Shocked, Dana whirled around to find the leader's irate face staring at her.

"You little bi…"

Before the man finished his statement, Dana snatched a rotted branch and smacked him in the head with it. His hand fell away from her. Quickly, she ran away from her captors and into the darkness.

Dana sped through the night. Scraggily branches scratched her face and tore at her clothes. She didn't care. She only wished to be away from them. Running blind, Dana forced herself onward, her heart racing within her chest.

Unsure of where she was headed, Dana kept running to put as much distance between her and those men. The last thing she wanted was for them to find her once they woke up. Twigs snapped and cracked as she ran.

Suddenly, the spindly trees ended, and once again, Dana found herself in the desert, except now tufts of dried grass poked through the sand. Sighing, she wondered if there was an end to this place and its dangers.

Dana stepped to her left. Instantly, her foot fell out from under her as the ledge she stood upon crumbled away. Tumbling, Dana rolled down a steep incline, picking up speed. She tucked her arms in hoping to prevent serious injury. Sharp pain gripped her lower side as she fell.

She crashed onto the bottom. Dazed, Dana lay still as

she tested her limbs. *Nothing broken.* Dana stood up. Searing pain gripped her lower leg the moment she put weight on it. Collapsing, Dana clutched it. Gingerly, she pulled up her pants leg. A huge gash lined it. Blood spurted from the wound as Dana put her hand on it.

She ripped off the uniform jacket. Carefully, Dana wrapped it around her leg to stem the bleeding. Tears welled in her eyes with each movement she made. With shaky hands, she tied her field dressing.

The dam broke. Tears she had held back all her life poured forth. Crying uncontrollably, Dana felt sorry for herself as the sense of abandonment settled in. She felt she had gone from one nightmare to another.

"George, why did you leave me?"

Only a soft breeze answered her. Dana heaved herself onto her feet and hobbled through the night determined to find help, or death.

CHAPTER

SEVEN

Sampson ignored the glaring sun as he worked in his field. With fluid movements, he raised his hoe and used it to hack the crust of the earth. Though most did not plant their fields at this time of year, Sampson always did. He put the roots of his plants deep within the ground and covered them with the moss that grew by the river.

Shuffling footsteps alerted him to a stranger's presence. Resting his hoe, Sampson looked up. A girl of about 17 years old stood before him. She wavered on her feet, barely able to stand. Sampson noted the blood-soaked bandage around her leg.

From her appearance, he judged that she had been wandering in the wilds for quite some time. Her tangled hair was caked with sand and mud. He approached her slowly, not wanting to frighten her.

"Kill me," she said in a hoarse whisper. "Kill me now."

The girl collapsed to the ground. Dropping his hoe, Sampson ran to her. "Minny!" he called.

A woman with dark skin and a purple apron tied around her waist stepped outside. "What is it?"

"Come here! Quick!"

Minny ran to her husband, the urgency in his voice worrying her. Her short, cropped hair bounced as she hurried over to him.

"My Lord," she gasped when she saw the unconscious teenager. "Get her in the house now."

Sampson lifted the girl into his arms and carried her to his home. Minny pointed to their bed before rushing out. She returned moments later with water and some cloth.

"What can I do?" asked Sampson.

"Get my stuff for sunburns and then stay out of the way," said Minny.

Sampson bowed to his wife. He rummaged through her box of medicine, finding the salve she used for burnt skin, and handed it to her. "I'll be just out the door if you need anything."

"Uh-huh," said Minny as she tended the stranger.

~ ~ ~

Colonel Fernau strode into the bustling room of computer terminals and clacking keyboards. A wall screen at the far end had satellite images zooming across it. In accordance with President Klens' orders, the number of drones used to spy on Dystopia's citizens had increased. The amount of information gathered had increased. All of which required more manpower. But this was not why Colonel Fernau had entered the intelligence room. Only one person concerned him.

He walked up to the first technician he saw. The young officer quivered before his presence, a fact that thrilled Colonel Fernau as he enjoyed instilling fear in others.

"May I help you, sir?" asked the man.

"Yes, you may," replied Colonel Fernau as he lovingly stroked his stick, something he was never without. "I need you to reposition a satellite for me."

"I cannot do that without authorization," said the man.

"I am your authorization," said Colonel Fernau, growing impatient.

"I'm sorry, sir," replied the young officer, "but only President Klens or the first councilman can give such authorization."

Irritated, Colonel Fernau struck the computer console with his stick. "I do not need authority from anyone."

"According to this, you do," said the man, hoping Colonel Fernau would not take his frustrations out on him.

"Your phone, now," said Colonel Fernau.

The young officer shakily handed it to him. Colonel Fernau snatched it. He dialed a number and tapped his foot as he waited for an answer. "Seth Michaels, please."

A moment passed.

"Mr. Michaels, do you or do you not want me to find Dana Ginary? Then give me the authorization to use the satellites and drones as I choose."

Colonel Fernau handed the phone to the officer. The poor man listened intently, shaking his head many times. After several minutes, he hung up, turning back to his computer.

"Do I have the authorization now?" asked Colonel Fernau, the sarcasm in his voice very prevalent.

"Yes, sir."

The young officer tapped away at the keys, bringing up window after window. "Which satellite do you want changed?"

"I want to spy on the wastelands where the known settlements are. Make certain that you pick up every detail." Colonel Fernau handed a picture of Dana to the man. "If she is spotted, you let me know immediately."

The young officer instantly entered all of the parameters into the computer. He scanned in Dana's image. The computer stored it, putting it up on the right side of the screen.

"One other thing," Colonel Fernau whispered into the man's ear. "Don't ever tell me I need authorization again."

The young officer nodded his head. Sweat formed on his brow as he wished that the colonel had chosen anyone but him. "Yes, sir."

Colonel Fernau stalked off. He whisked out of the computer room and down the hallway with its bluish lights.

CHAPTER EIGHT

Dana's eye's fluttered open as she regained consciousness. She glanced around her strange, new surroundings. The soft bed that enveloped her body amazed Dana. She had never known anything could be so comfortable.

Scuffling sounds just outside the room drew her attention. She tried to sit up. Weak and disoriented, Dana threw her hand out to steady herself, knocking items off the bedside table. They clattered on the floor, making more noise than she wanted.

A plump, dark woman hurried in with a tray of food. "Good to see you finally awake," she said. She put the tray down and helped Dana into a sitting position.

Dana slumped against the pillows, too weak to hold herself up. "Who are you?"

"Name's Minny," said the cheerful woman as she placed

the tray in Dana's lap. "Now eat up. You've had quite an ordeal and need to put some meat on them bones."

"Pardon?"

"You're too skinny. Now eat up. If you need anything, just holler."

Minny left the room and went about her daily tasks.

Dana studied the tray of food and its contents: buttered toast, bacon, eggs, sausage, an apple, an orange, hollandaise sauce, and a sprig of mint. She couldn't believe the amount of food. Never in her life had she been allowed to have so much in one sitting.

Minny returned. She stopped, stared at Dana's still full plate, and put her hands on her hips. "Why, you haven't eaten one bite. Now I know there isn't anything wrong with my cooking, so there must be a problem with your appetite."

"I've… I've never been allowed to eat food like this before," said Dana.

Minny pulled up a chair. "What do you mean, honey?"

"Where I come from," said Dana, "such food is forbidden. Deemed unhealthy."

"You mean Dystopia," said Minny. "Honey, Sampson and I knew you were from there the moment we first saw you. Your clothes kind of gave it away."

Minny pointed to the uniform that Dana had put on to help George escape. "We found these as well," Minny said as she handed Dana the locket and disk.

Dana quickly put them around her neck. "Thank you."

"Well, you eat up," said Minny, "No one's going to stop you from having a full stomach here."

Dana speared a sausage and took a bite. Instantly, her

mouth filled with saliva as she savored the taste, glad to be able to eat something. It took her close to an hour to finish. When she had, Minny took the tray and made Dana rest some more.

Several days passed as Dana recovered from being lost in the wasteland. The cut on her leg healed nicely.

"Wasn't so bad," Minny had said one day when she changed the bandage, "Just needed attention. You should be able to walk on it now."

Dana heaved herself up. Gingerly, she put her weight on her leg. It still smarted, but not so bad. Limping, she managed to walk across the room without too much trouble.

"Here," Minny handed Dana a walking stick. "Sampson!"

Sampson walked into the room.

"Why don't you take Dana here for a walk in the sunshine? Show her around."

"Woman, you know I got work to do."

Minny gave Sampson a menacing stare.

"Getting the truck right now."

Within the hour, Dana and Sampson rode out to the fields he owned. She couldn't believe how vast the space was. "How much sand is out here?"

"More than you can imagine."

"And how much of it are you allowed to work on?"

Sampson looked at her funny. "Allowed? I own it. From that fence there to about five miles in that direction is my land. It's mine to do with as I please.

"I plow it, plant it, and harvest it. I hire people from time to time to help me out, but the land and its contents are mine."

Dana couldn't believe it. "You mean, no one comes in and tells you what to do with it?"

"Nope," said Sampson, "And if they dare try, they can argue with my little friend here." Sampson patted his shotgun.

Dana looked at it in horror. Back home, only the officers were allowed to carry weapons. "Aren't you afraid of getting into trouble by carrying that thing?"

"Nope," replied Sampson. "Why shouldn't I be allowed to? It's my right to defend myself. You see, out here are all sorts of wild animals. We still have thieves and bandits that roam through here. They used to steal my crops until I killed one of them for trying. Now they stay clear of me and I prefer it that way."

"And you weren't punished for murder?" People who killed someone for breaking in their home in Dystopia were arrested and never heard from again.

"Why should I be? The man trespassed on my land and was making off with my harvest. He had no right to it."

Confused, Dana just sat in silence as the beat-up pickup rocked back and forth as it bounced along.

"Here. I'll show you something." Sampson pulled the truck to a halt. He and Dana got out, and he led her to a place with clear plastic plating on the ground.

"This is one of five greenhouses," said Sampson. "It took me 10 years, but I built them into the ground like this to protect them from the weather. As you can see, the land is trying to come back from whatever turned it into a desert in the first place."

Sampson pointed at some green tufts of grass.

"But I can't rely on the weather and we need food year round, so I made five underground greenhouses. This plastic ceiling is 10 inches thick to block out the elements. However, you will note that you can see right through it. So it lets the sunlight in.

"I have the professor to thank for that. He even made it so that I could block out the excess sun during the summer months." Sampson pressed a button on a control pad. Instantly, the plastic fogged up.

Dana studied the mechanism. She had never seen one like it before. "Don't the plants need water?"

"Yes, ma'am, they do," replied Sampson. "There is an underground river that goes through here. I drilled into it and set up an irrigation system, using the river water to water my plants. I control how much they get so they are never over or under watered. And this plastic ceiling opens up when I want to ventilate the greenhouse."

He pressed another button and slits appeared in the plastic covering.

Ingenious, thought Dana. "How can the river be underground? I thought they were always above ground."

"Most rivers are, but sometimes they end up underground. There have been instances of sinkholes forming near a river. When that happens, it and everything around it falls into the earth until it is completely covered. The river I tapped into is the Platte River."

"Oh."

"This is an orchard here," said Sampson. "I have an orange field in another, and the remaining three are full of various vegetables."

"You were plowing your fields above ground when I arrived."

"Yep," said Sampson. "I plant stuff in the ground as well to hold the dirt down. If I get anything worthwhile from them, I sell it as well.

"I've been planting various grasses and plants over there

that are indigenous to the area. Figure it might help cut down on the dust storms we get."

Dana looked around the sand-ridden expanse. She had been told stories about what caused this area to become barren, but they were the government approved stories. "What happened here?"

"No one really knows," said Sampson. "It happened so long ago. I found some material in the library dating back to that time. People blamed it on the wrath of God. Some blamed man-made global warming. One group actually thought that the apocalypse was coming and decided to prepare themselves through rituals of purification. Another group blames capitalism. The blame goes on from there."

"But man's greed is the cause of many of our troubles," said Dana, repeating a line from her textbook.

"And did your schools in that area teach you that?"

Dana nodded.

"Spend enough time working the land and you'll learn that no human being can dictate the weather. I figure all this happened because Mother Nature saw fit to put us back in our place.

"Whatever the cause, it doesn't matter. What matters is how we deal with the situation. One thing I do know is that one day the rains stopped coming and the land dried up. But these last several years, I have noticed an increase in the amount of rain. So maybe this will become fertile once again."

"How do you get in there?" asked Dana, pointing at the greenhouse.

"There's a door right over there. It leads to a staircase that takes you down. Not going there today though.

"Well, time to get going." Sampson led Dana back to the truck.

She opened the squeaky door and climbed in. Sampson put it in drive and steered the vehicle back to the town.

"Minny and I live just outside the town, but not too far. It ain't a big place, but we like it here."

"What's the name of the town?" asked Dana.

"We call it Libre," said Sampson. "It's a great place to make a new life."

Sampson slowed the truck. He pulled out some binoculars and used them to study the horizon in the distance.

"What is it?" asked Dana.

"A group of people are approaching town." He reached for his weapon.

Dana squinted into the distance. All she saw were black specks.

"Ah, they're just traders." Sampson released his hold on his gun.

"Traders?"

"Yeah," said Sampson. "People who come through here with things we need. They travel to the ruins that surround us and bring back anything of value for which we trade for. For a moment, I thought they were a party of bandits, but they're not."

"What would happen if they were bandits?" asked Dana.

Sampson looked at his shotgun before answering. "Nothing good."

They rolled into the town of Libre soon after. Many passersby waved at Sampson as he and Dana drove through the town.

"Morning, Mayor," greeted one man.

"Mayor?" asked Dana.

"Oh, yeah," said Sampson. "Almost forgot to tell you. I'm the mayor of this town. And Ross there is the sheriff."

"Sheriff?"

"Our law enforcement. Most people settle their own differences around here, but every so often, we have need of a sheriff."

Dana glanced around at the streets bustling with activity. Stores and shops stood proudly with their signs. People went in and out of the shops at will. One man pushed a cart down the walk.

"Hot dogs! Fresh hot dogs!"

Dana watched as a child walked up to him and bought a hot dog. Amazed, she couldn't believe that he just ate it right there in public.

"Where are the officers?"

"The what? Oh, yeah, forgot where you're from. No officers around here. We formed our own police force. Mostly, folk just band together when necessary. Our sheriff was elected, and when the time comes, both he and I will have to face re-election."

"Elected? You actually choose your leaders?"

"Well, yeah." Sampson pulled the truck to the side of the road and parked. "This is a good spot to walk around."

Dana got out, using her walking stick to support herself. She found she was walking more easily, but didn't want to overdo it.

"Hot dog?" The man with the hot dog cart looked at her questioningly.

"Uh, I don't have any money," said Dana.

"No problem," said the man. "Have one on the house. If you like it, then you can pay me for the next one."

He handed her a hot dog in a soft bun. Dana took it, unsure of how to eat it.

"Ketchup? Mustard?"

"Uh, sure," said Dana.

The hot dog man put some ketchup and mustard on her hot dog. Carefully, Dana took a bite, getting the ketchup all over her face.

Sampson burst out laughing. "Ain't ever had one of those, have you?"

Mortified, Dana grabbed a napkin and wiped her mouth. Surprisingly, she liked the hot dog. "So, this is your cart?"

"Yep," said the man. "Set it up a week ago."

"That quick? Permits usually take months to get approved."

"Permits? Oh, you're not from around here. I don't need a permit. Why should any man need a permit to start a business? Nope, I saved up until I had enough money to buy the items I needed and set up shop."

"You enjoy your hot dog, now. I'm here most days if you want more." The man walked off to sell more of his stock.

"What about food safety?" asked Dana to Sampson.

"If he sells a bad product, he goes out of business."

Dana had never thought about that. Then she remembered what the milkman had told her once about how cooked manure was still manure. She shoved the remaining hot dog into her mouth.

"If someone wants to start a shop, they can," said Sampson. "If they wish to work for someone else, they can do that too. Plenty of folk have work that needs doing. If we have disputes, there is a board—its members elected—which mediate those disputes."

"So, you live as you choose," said Dana.

"Precisely," said Sampson. "We have agreed to live according to a certain set of rules, but our lives are our own."

"Says you." A man swaggered up to Dana and Sampson with a bottle in his hands. His slurred speech told Dana he was drunk. "I've been stuck in this cesspool forever."

"No one's keeping you here," snapped Sampson, the disdain prevalent in his voice.

"Well, I don't got money to get out," said the man.

"Dana, meet Bert, the town drunk."

"Spare me a coin?" asked Bert.

Dana backed away from his foul-smelling breath.

"Get out of here," said Sampson.

"Won't even give me anything," muttered Bert.

"You wouldn't need anything if you'd quit drinking and learn to work for a living," said Sampson. He steered Dana away. "Bert is one of those people who feels he ought to just be given the things he wants out of life."

Dana watched as Bert staggered away, talking to himself.

"What are your skills?" asked Sampson.

"What?" The question surprised Dana.

"We got to find you a job," said Sampson. "You can't keep living at my place. Well, we can rent a room to you."

"I don't really have any skills." Dana had never had to think about it.

"What did you do back in Dystopia?"

"Waste Management. It was decided for me."

Sampson rubbed his hand over his chin. "I think I know where you can start. Betsy here has an eatery. She's getting on in years and could use the help. You can work there a bit and earn some money. After that, you can decide what you want to do."

They walked over to Betsy's diner. It was a simple place

with a counter, stools, and the grill right behind it. Dana marveled at the place.

"Hey, mayor," said Betsy. "Who's this?"

"Dana, and she needs a job."

"I don't need any help," said Betsy.

"Now, look here. You know you're having trouble doing some of the harder tasks. She can help you. And I know you got more than enough to afford to pay her."

"Can you clean?" asked Betsy.

"Yes," said Dana.

"Can you cook?" asked Betsy.

"No," said Dana.

"How do you feed yourself?"

"Now, Betsy, you take it easy on her."

"Fine," said Betsy. "I'll pay you 250 a week."

"Four hundred," said Dana. She had no idea where that came from or why she blurted it out.

"Well, the girl knows how to negotiate. Three seventy-five."

Dana decided not to push her luck. "Done."

"Fine. Report to work in the morning."

Dana and Sampson walked out. Sampson noticed the downhearted look on her face.

"You don't have to work there the rest of your life," he said. "Just long enough to figure out what you want to do and get on your feet. No one here is going to force you to do anything you don't want."

Dana smiled.

They walked back to his truck and got in. Once again, she glanced at his gun.

"You ever handle one of those?"

"No. It was forbidden."

"Think I'll take you out sometime and show you how. Though we're pretty safe here in the town, every so often, unsavory folk come about."

Dana thought back to the bandits that had kidnapped her. She hoped she never met them again.

"A person ought to know how to defend themselves." Sampson steered the truck up a hill. "I think it's time you met Karl."

Dana watched the buildings pass the windows as they drove through town. Sampson expertly steered them from one road to another until he reached a small neighborhood of houses that seemed to be well-built, or at least constructed better that Dana would have believed possible.

When they reached one with charred siding, Sampson stopped. He parked the truck on the side of the road. "That is Karl's place. You can usually tell his because it stands out with its uniquely decorated siding. Come on."

Dana hopped out of the vehicle. She followed Sampson up to the door of the house. She fidgeted slightly as he knocked.

"Now, Karl is a bit eccentric, but there isn't anything you need to fear from him," said Sampson as they waited for someone to answer the door. "Just don't let him talk you into helping with any of his projects."

"Projects?"

"He is constantly building something, which usually blows something up."

The door ripped open. Before them stood an old man with wild hair and goggles on his face, which made his eyes look huge. Black smudges covered his pasty face. "Sampson, come on in."

The door widened as Sampson and Dana entered. The cluttered house had papers and books everywhere. Only one chair remained uncovered. Dana figured that was where Karl spent most of his time. A workbench was in the next room. On it was some weird machine that she couldn't identify.

"Who's this?" Karl asked, pointing at Dana.

"Dana," replied Sampson. "She's new in town and I thought I would introduce the two of you."

"You just wanted to show her the crazy mad scientist of the town."

"Something like that," said Sampson.

"What's this?" asked Dana, indicating a big cylinder about waist high, shaking and rumbling.

"My washing machine," said Karl. "Made it myself." He opened the lid and pulled out some soggy socks.

"Oh," said Dana.

"But this over here is more interesting." Karl led her to another room. In it was a homemade computer terminal with wires leading from it, buzzing with electricity.

"What is it?" asked Dana.

"This is my homemade communication system," replied Karl. "I hacked into the satellite network of the Dystopian government. Now I can bring up all of their broadcasts and communications."

"You what?" asked Sampson. "Are you insane? You'll lead them right to us."

"They won't even know," said Karl, waving away Sampson's concerns.

Sampson snorted.

"And over here," Karl grabbed Dana's hand and led her to another part of his house, "is my indoor garden. I got these specialized UV lights—made them myself—hooked up here for the plants. My own irrigation system goes through here and waters the plants. It's all on timers. It's all very clean and neat. And because it's indoors, I don't need to worry about the weather."

"Neat compared to the rest of your house," muttered Sampson.

"Oh, who cares about cleaning house when there are more important things to do?" Karl bounced around as he continued to show off his various inventions. Amazed, Dana just looked around, barely able to take it all in, wondering how he managed to create it all. She reached out to touch an ornate box.

"Stay away from that!" Karl seized her and yanked her back, just as the box opened and snapped shut.

"What was that?" demanded Dana as she tried to catch her breath.

"Mouse trap," said Karl.

"Rule number one," whispered Sampson to Dana, "Touch nothing. You never know what might bite back."

Dana counted her fingers, making certain all of them remained.

"Well, Karl," said Sampson, "we appreciate you letting us visit, but now we must go. There is a lot of stuff we need to do."

"Oh, okay." Karl's face fell.

"We'll be back," said Sampson.

"Alright," Karl's face brightened. "I get so few visitors."

"I wonder why," Sampson whispered to Dana.

"Thanks, Karl," said Dana as she left, "for showing me your home."

"Come by anytime. My door is always open."

Dana waved good-bye and limped after Sampson out the door. They headed down the walk to his truck.

"So what'd you think?" asked Sampson.

"He's nice," said Dana.

Sampson laughed. "That's Karl. Strange, but nice. He's a good man and he knows his stuff. Anyway, whether you decide to visit or not is up to you. I just figured you ought to meet." Sampson held the passenger door open for Dana. "Well, it's time we head back. Minny will be worrying about what's happened to us."

~ ~ ~

Colonel Fernau drummed his fingers on his desk, staring at a picture of Dana Ginary. Rage filled him. She had humiliated him once too often, and he vowed to get even. No one ever embarrassed him and got away with it.

A knock sounded and a female officer walked in. "The requisition reports you asked for."

He snatched them from her hands.

The woman noticed the picture of Dana. "Pardon me, sir, but you have been staring at the photo for weeks. Don't you think it's time to move on to other things?"

In response to her question, Colonel Fernau grabbed his stick and smacked her across the face with it, knocking her to the ground. He rose from his chair and paced around the frightened officer as she looked up at him. Without a word, he raised his stick and struck her repeatedly until she no longer moved.

"No," Colonel Fernau's callous voice terrified even the cockroaches in the room.

Two more officers charged in, having heard the commotion.

"Take this filth out of here," said Colonel Fernau as he

wiped the blood from his switch, "and find me a new secretary. Preferably one who won't ask annoying questions."

Too frightened to disobey, the two officers rushed to the still body on the floor and dragged it away.

Colonel Fernau approached the photo of Dana hanging on his wall. "Dana Ginary, wherever you are, I will find you. And I will break you."

He paced to the other side of his office before yanking out his knife and chucking it at the picture, striking Dana's photo in the face. A vindictive smile crept across his face as he retrieved his knife.

~ ~ ~

Dana sat in a rocking chair on the porch. She moved it back and forth as she stared at the vast stars in the sky while holding George's locket. She wished he were here.

"Am I intruding?" asked Minny as she walked out onto the porch.

"No," said Dana.

"A friend of yours?" Minny pointed at the locket in Dana's hand.

"Yes."

"He live around here?"

"No, he's dead," said Dana.

"I'm sorry," said Minny. "You know, sometimes when a person has a lot on their mind, it helps if they talk about it."

"I'm fine, really."

"He meant a great deal to you."

"His name was George," said Dana. "He looked out

for me at the plant. I never appreciated it until now. But I betrayed him. They made me do it. Your parents or your friend, that was the choice they offered me.

"I betrayed my friend to save my parents, but they were already dead. I betrayed George for my own selfishness."

Tears streamed down Dana's cheeks. Minny reached out and comforted her, holding her close.

"There, there," soothed Minny, patting Dana's back. "It isn't selfishness to want to save your family. You love them."

"But George is dead because of me."

"Honey, I don't think that's true. Those men you spoke of, they forced you to make a terrible choice, one no one should ever have to make. They are the selfish ones."

"But he'll never know how sorry I am. I wish I could take it back."

"Hindsight does that to us," said Minny. "Learn from this. Don't play their game next time."

"But George died thinking that I am a horrible person. And he's right."

"That isn't true. Did he give you the locket?"

"Yes," said Dana, sniffling. "It belonged to his wife before she died. He carried it with him always. Then, right before they killed him, he gave it to me. 'Live for the both of us,' he said."

"Then, honey, I think he knew you loved him. He knew you were forced to hurt him. And he forgave you."

"How do you know?"

"He wouldn't have given you that locket if he hadn't."

Dana stared at the tarnished gold plating of the locket with new eyes.

"You should say good-bye to him and honor his memory. Out there in the field are a lot of rocks. Write George's name on one and stick it on the ground."

"It won't bring him back," sobbed Dana.

"No, it won't," conceded Minny, "but it will help you to say farewell to a friend and move on. It's something we all must do."

Dana wiped her tears with her hand.

"Here," said Minny, handing her a handkerchief.

Dana sniffed and smiled shyly as she took it. "Thanks."

"Now you go on and say your good-byes."

Clutching the locket tightly, Dana walked out into the field and searched the ground. She strolled by several rocks. None of them seemed good enough to be George's memorial. She spotted one. Picking it up, Dana brushed the dirt and grit off it. *Perfect.*

She scratched George's name into it and placed it carefully on the ground by some bushes. Gingerly, Dana scooped dirt around it to hold it. Once finished, she stood up.

"To George," said Dana. "To the man who saved my life."

Dana pulled out the locket and started to place it around the rock. She stopped. Unable to part with it, she put it back around her neck, took one last look at the stone, and left.

Morning dawned on Dana's third week in Libre as she reported for work at Betsy's diner. She tied an apron around her waist and poured coffee for the first customer. A group of weather-worn men walked in and settled into a couple of booths. Immediately, Dana grabbed a pot of freshly brewed coffee and filled cups for them.

"You must be new here," said one of the men.

"Yes," said Dana.

"In that case, we'll all take some specials."

Dana smiled and went back to the kitchen. "Seven specials."

"I know. I know," came Betsy's crabby response. "Those traders always get the special."

"Traders?" asked Dana.

"Yeah. They're the ones who come through here every now and then with stuff to trade that they've found from Lord knows where."

Interested, Dana decided to keep an eye on them. She had heard about the traders around town, and the idea of living an independent life free from the constraints of society thrilled her. Though she didn't mind the steady work at the diner and she received more respect there than at Waste Management, Dana wanted to do something more.

"Order up!"

Dana grabbed the plate of food and set it before the lone man at the counter. Casually, she walked over to the traders and the man who had placed the orders. They chatted in a language unfamiliar to her.

"Excuse me," said Dana, "do you know this place that is northeast of here? It is a ruined city with all sorts of tall, crumbling buildings."

"Yes, we know it," said the man who had spoken before. "Why do you ask?"

"I got lost in there when I was lost in the wasteland," replied Dana.

"You must be that new girl everyone is talking about," said the man. "My name is Malcolm, and these guys, well, their names aren't important."

"Dana."

"How do you like working here? We come here every time we stop in town."

"It's all right," said Dana.

"Dana, get on back here. These plates won't carry themselves out," came Betsy's voice from the kitchen.

Groaning, Dana retrieved the tray of completed orders and carried them out to the traders.

"You could come with us," said Malcolm.

"Really? You don't mind?"

"We always welcome new traders," said Malcolm. "Get yourself a horse and some provisions for a long trip through the barren lands and you will be welcome to join us. We'll be back through this way in about three weeks. If you have your gear by then, you are welcome to come with us. We'll make sure to bring you back."

Dana eyed the smiling faces around her. She nearly jumped at the chance. Betsy's crassness wore on her, and she wanted to do something different for a change, something of her own choosing. "How much does a horse cost?"

"You'll have to work that out with Mr. Callors," replied Malcolm. "He owns the stable down the road here. But I'm sure he'll work something out with you."

"Thank you," said Dana, thrilled at being able to do something spontaneous.

Betsy's drumming fingers caught her attention. "I better get back to work." She ran back to the kitchen area for more finished orders.

"So, you've been here three weeks and already you are plotting your departure," said Betsy.

Dana looked at the woman with wide eyes unsure of how to answer.

"Oh, don't give me that look, child," Betsy waved her hand, "I'm an old crank, but I know that you young people like to have your moments of adventure. No one stays here for long. That's how I like it."

"So, you don't mind if I take some time to travel with them?"

"No, go ahead. This diner will always be here."

Ecstatic, Dana rushed off with the plates.

"Mind you, it's temporary work. You'll need something to do when you return."

"I could work here during those times," said Dana.

"What makes you think I want you?" said Betsy, her mouth twitched in a tight smile.

"What makes you think you have a choice?" Dana retorted.

"Go on and serve those platters before the food gets cold and the customer complains."

Grinning, Dana rushed out with the orders and placed them before the respective customers. Her mind raced with the possibilities of being able to see a new world and follow her own mind.

CHAPTER

NINE

Elsie and Sanders moved carefully through the city, trying not to attract attention. When the riot at the plant started, they fled, knowing exactly what the outcome would be. Since then, they were forced to stay on the move to avoid capture. Fleeing your career assignment resulted in being arrested and disappearing.

They spotted an officer up ahead. Casually, Elsie steered Sanders away from him and down another street. Clinging to each other, they trotted down the sidewalk.

On a screen above them was Dana's picture with the words terrorist, traitor, anarchist, and murderer. Elsie frowned. For weeks, they had been airing reports about Dana's crimes. She hoped her friend found a safe place to hide out.

"Here," said Sanders, finding an unlocked door to a seemingly abandoned building.

They went inside. Looking around, Elsie and Sanders

found that no one had lived in that place for a while. The scattered items told them that whoever had occupied it before had been arrested.

"We should be safe here for a while," said Elsie.

"But for how long?" replied Sanders.

She didn't have an answer. Elsie had no idea how long they could keep running before they were caught. "Maybe we should search for the resistance," she said.

"They don't exist anymore."

"I'm not so sure about that. If that was the case, then why are they trying so hard to find Dana? They seem to think that she was a central figure within the movement."

"But can we trust them?" asked Sanders.

"I don't know. But I do know that if we keep going as we have been, we'll get caught eventually, and you know what our fate will be."

Sanders relented.

"Come on," said Elsie. "Let's see if there's anything to eat around here." She shivered.

"You cold?" asked Sanders, with concern in his voice.

"It's nothing."

"Here." Sanders gingerly put his arm around Elsie's shoulders, pulling her close until their bodies met. "Better?"

"Much. Thank you." Elsie snuggled into Sanders' shoulder. "You know, you're really not such a geek."

"And you're smarter than you are pretty," said Sanders.

"So I'm not beautiful?" Elsie jerked her head up and stared at Sanders with a mildly hurt expression.

"No… you are… it's just… you're…" Sanders cut himself off when he noticed Elsie's playful smile. "You had me there."

They laughed as Elsie settled her head back on Sanders'

shoulder. Together, they remained in the dismal home while they waited for morning, comforted in one another's embrace.

~ ~ ~

The sound of the gunshot echoed across the plains. Dana's shoulder hurt slightly from the shotgun's recoil. She rubbed it to ease the soreness.

"Not bad," said Sampson, "but you missed the target."

Dana glared at him. She knew she had missed the target. She was just glad to not have accidentally shot herself.

"Here," Sampson took the gun from her, "hold it like this." He demonstrated how to properly handle the weapon. "You hold it snug against your shoulder, but not too tightly. Also, hold it straight. Use the sights to aim. Let your breath out before you fire, and squeeze the trigger gently."

Dana carefully took the shotgun again. She held it like Sampson had shown her. Lining it up, Dana fired. Once again, the noise reverberated around her. Dana glanced at the target. She had nicked it.

"Well, it's an improvement," said Sampson, handing her a few more shells. "With a fair amount of practice, you should be able to hit its center."

Dana reloaded the gun and fired again. Each time she tried, her aim improved, but still wasn't accurate.

"So, how's work at the eatery?"

"Fine," said Dana.

"Thought about what you're going to do after?" asked Sampson.

Dana had thought about it. "Thought I'd see about joining the traders. I've got enough money to buy my own horse and supplies."

"The traders?" Sampson eyed her pensively. "What for?"

"I need to learn the area," said Dana. "I've been talking with Malcolm. He said that I am welcome to join his band when they come through again."

"I don't much care for the idea of you going off with them alone," said Sampson.

"I don't want to continue working for Betsy."

Sampson laughed. "She is a bit crass. I still don't like the idea of you going alone."

"I won't be alone."

Sampson eyed her suspiciously.

"I'm going," said Dana.

"Very well," said Sampson. "Then I'm coming with you."

"What about your farm here?" asked Dana.

"I have enough employees who can tend the fields. Besides, at this time of year, there isn't much that needs doing."

"But you're the mayor."

"True, but that doesn't mean that I have to be here all the time. Malcolm is a good man and he'll look after you, but I would feel more comfortable if I went along. At least until you learn how to shoot properly and navigate your own way around these parts."

Dana relented. She had learned by now that when Sampson made up his mind, there was no arguing against it.

~ ~ ~

"You wished to see me, father," said Kenny as he entered his father's study.

Seth Michaels glanced up at his son from the papers on his

desk. "Yes. One of the rail lines seems to have fallen into disrepair. Either way, we are unable to get trains through, which means we cannot get our resources through. A crew is being sent out to repair the line and I want you to monitor them."

"Monitor them?"

"Yes," said Seth Michaels. "It will be good training for you."

"Yes, sir," said Kenny. He had no desire to leave home.

"I know it is not the most ideal assignment," said his father, "but someone has to do it, and it is time for you to know just how barbaric the outside world is. Besides, if you can manage this task, then I know that you are fit for this job.

"It will only be for a few weeks. Then you will be back here."

"Father, what line is in need of repair?" asked Kenny.

His father looked at him curiously a moment. "Why the oil and coal line."

Kenny was surprised at that answer. "I thought we had abandoned the use of oil and coal in favor of something more environmentally friendly."

"Kenny, don't be so naïve," laughed his father. "How do you think we are able to heat this house in the winter? The solar panels on the roof don't even work. They're simply for show."

"What about the resource shortage?" Kenny had heard his whole life how resources were limited and must be conserved.

"There is a resource shortage because we made it that way. President Klens felt it best to keep resources limited in order to keep the populace under control. We don't need them rioting again. There is more than enough oil to heat every home in Dystopia, but it is best that it remains in our control, as we are the only ones who know how to use it properly."

"Yes, father," said Kenny.

"Now, you will leave in the morning for your assignment. Keep the workers under control and get the line working again, and you will be back home before you know it."

Seth Michaels hugged his son in an unusually affectionate embrace. Kenny allowed it to happen. He refused to think much about it and assumed his father was missing his absence already. A small prick tickled his shoulder. Quickly, Kenny glanced at it, but his father pushed him away, forcing his gaze forward.

"I will miss you, boy," said Seth Michaels. "But I know you will handle it and be back before we've had time to miss one another."

"Thank you, father," said Kenny.

Kenny left his father to prepare for his journey. Some of his father's statements concerned him, but he shrugged them off. He had never gone without comfort.

~ ~ ~

For the second time in a week, Colonel Fernau entered the intelligence gathering room with all of its computers and images from various government controlled satellites and drones. He had received a phone call from the place about a possible match to Dana's photo. His boots clicked on the floor as he marched over to the man in charge of the area. "You called?"

"Yes, colonel," said the supervisor, as he tugged at his wrinkled uniform. "We have two possible matches to that Ginary girl." The man punched a few keys on the computer. Up popped two recently recorded images from the satellite. "This is the first one."

He enlarged the picture. Colonel Fernau studied it a moment. The chin seemed the same, but the stature did not match Dana. Always having an eye for detail, Colonel Fernau never forgot the physical features of anyone he met. That was part of what made him so good at his job, besides the fact that he loved tormenting people.

"It's not her," he growled.

The man clicked on the second image, enlarging it so that it filled the screen. Colonel Fernau studied it. Same hair and chin. Though it was more of a shot of her head, the girl in the picture fit Dana's characteristics. "Can you enlarge it further?"

The man tapped a few keys and the picture blew up to where it filled the entire screen in the front of the monitoring room.

Approaching the view screen with a computer pad in his hands, Colonel Fernau highlighted certain aspects of the photo. His piercing eyes studied every inch of it, his face growing more wrathful with each passing second. Not her either.

"She's not the one," he slammed the computer pad on a nearby desk, causing the poor woman sitting there to jump in fright. "I want her found, do you understand? I don't care what it takes or how many hours you have to devote to this. Find me that girl!"

The man frowned, knowing that this meant spending what little free time he had looking for Colonel Fernau's newest obsession.

"Where is this place?" asked Colonel Fernau, pointing at a satellite image of a group of roads and buildings.

"Some settlement out in the barren wasteland. There are a few of them."

"I want you to find out which one."

"Yes, sir."

"I want you to reroute some drones to this area." Colonel Fernau's innate sense at finding people kicked in.

"We have several drones out there now, sir. I can send one or two to this area."

"Do it," ordered Colonel Fernau. "Make certain that the drones will not be detected by the people living there. I do not want them alerted to our spying on them. She is out there, somewhere. Maybe a drone will have better luck in finding her, since its abilities are not subject to the whims of emotion."

"Colonel… I… I assure you," stammered the poor supervisor.

"Save it," snapped Colonel Fernau. "If Dana Ginary is not found, I will be holding you personally responsible, understand?"

"Yes, sir," said the man, hoping to never meet Colonel Fernau again.

"Good." Colonel Fernau turned on his heels and marched out of the room, reveling in the fear that he had instilled in the room.

CHAPTER

TEN

Dana leaned on the fence to the corral as she watched the horses wander about, grazing on the bits of grass that grew there. Money bulged from her pocket. Excitement filled her as she thought about the horse she would buy. Her mind raced with all of the possibilities of owning a horse and the things she would be able to do.

"Dana?"

She turned around and greeted the man that had walked up behind her.

"I am Mr. Callors, the owner of this place."

"Pleased to meet you." Dana shook his hand.

"So you want to buy a horse?"

"Yes. I hope to join the traders the next time they pass through here."

"A future trader, eh? Well, you'll need a good one. Do you know anything about horses?"

Dana shook her head.

"Well there's time for me to teach you the basics. You'll learn fast enough. It isn't' hard. Mostly, you have to feed it, give it plenty of water, exercise it, and keep the stall clean. Now I can take care of the feeding and cleaning if you wish for a fee. At least until you get more accustomed to having a horse."

"You will?"

"Yep. I provide lodging for horses if a person has a mind to keep it in my stables. You pay monthly for the room and board. Now as for your horse."

Mr. Callors motioned for Dana to follow him. He headed for the horses in the corral and picked up the reins of one. "This one here is Nell. She's very mild tempered and has no trouble with the desert. Do ya, girl?"

Dana watched as Mr. Callors stroked the horse's muzzle. The snorting of another caught her attention. A young horse trotted about, prancing back and forth with pride. He shook his mane and snorted some more. Enthralled, Dana watched the horse put on a little show for her as though he were trying to tell her what a great animal he was. He pranced some more, only stopping to paw at the ground a bit.

Dana liked him immediately. "What about that one?"

Mr. Callors looked where she pointed. "He's only two years old. Still got a lot to learn. I only just taught him to accept a rider. Bought him off a trader recently. Haven't even named him yet."

The horse strutted before her, neighing merrily. Before Dana knew it, she found herself growing attached to the animal as he showed off. "His name is Poboy."

"Poboy?"

"He looks like a Poboy," said Dana, afraid she might have overstepped her bounds.

Mr. Callors laughed. His delighted guffaws made Dana wonder if she had done something wrong. "You went and named him."

"What does that matter?" asked Dana.

"Once you name it, you'll never want another. Well, Poboy it is. He's young like you. Perhaps you can learn about the world together.

"Now, mind you, a horse is more than just an animal. Poboy will become your friend. Having a horse is a commitment. You and Poboy will be spending a lot of time together from now until you leave with the traders."

Mr. Callors grabbed Poboy and guided him over to Dana. The horse trotted to her, head held high. Carefully, Dana took the reins. She raised her hand and slowly placed it on the horse's muzzle. Gently, her fingers brushed the short fur. Poboy shook his head and nuzzled into her.

"He likes you all right," laughed Mr. Callors. "Well, time to learn to ride."

He retrieved a saddle from a hook on the wall and brought it over. Dana listened intently as he explained how to strap it onto the horse, watching all of his movements. Once done, she allowed him to help her into the saddle.

"I'll guide him first until you get used to sitting in there."

For the next hour, Mr. Callors walked around the corral, leading Poboy and Dana. She allowed her body motion to synchronize with the movements of the horse. After about 15 minutes, Dana had become saddle sore, but she refused to say anything.

Before they had finished, Mr. Callors handed the reins

to her, explaining how to get the horse to go where she wanted him to. "Tug them the right a bit. Gentle now."

Dana did so. Immediately, Poboy turned right.

"To the left."

Dana gently pulled the reins to the left, amazed at how Poboy quickly switched direction.

"If you want to stop, pull back a bit."

Dana did so. Poboy halted. He looked up at her as though he wondered why she had stopped.

"Now, gently nudge him with your heels to go forward."

Dana bumped the animal's side with her heels. Poboy started walking at a fast trot, pleased that she had decided to keep going.

"I think you got it," said Mr. Callors. "Time to feed and brush him."

Dana steered Poboy to the stables and dismounted. The horse touched her with his nose, jostling her a bit. Smiling, Dana turned around and petted him.

"I think you two will get along just fine," said Mr. Callors, handing her a brush. "Now, you have to groom him regularly. Nice even strokes."

Dana removed the saddle and copied his movements. Poboy neighed with delight. Though her arm tired, she enjoyed grooming her horse. Poboy had a lot of personality, something Dana enjoyed.

"You're a fast learner," said Mr. Callors.

Dana handed him the brush when she had finished.

"Feeding is pretty simple. All of the horse feed is in this bin. Put one scoop into the trough there. That is Poboy's stall. The water trough is there. I use the hose to keep it filled. Rakes are over there in that closet. Use one of them when you clean out the manure. You might not have to do that too often. I usually hire someone to clean out the stalls."

"That's it?" asked Dana.

"Pretty much. It's the basics. But the main thing Poboy here needs is love and care. Make sure you visit him often. Every day if you can. At least three or four times a week. Horses, like people, can get lonely. You need to visit him often and ride him often so that he remains used to your presence.

"If the stable is ever locked, there's a key under the bucket outside. You can use that to let yourself in. Just make sure you lock up afterwards."

"Yes, Mr. Callors."

"Well, young lady, you got yourself a horse. I'm here most every day. The corral out there is perfect for riding. When you get more ambitious, you can take him out on the property here."

"Thank you," said Dana.

"Be here in the morning," said Mr. Callors as he locked up. "We'll have another lesson about the care of horses then."

Dana darted off, waving good-bye. The bulging pocket reminded her that she had forgotten to pay. "Mr. Callors! We forgot to settle on a price."

"We'll settle tomorrow."

Thrilled about having a horse of her own, Dana thanked him and ran off.

~ ~ ~

Steam billowed from the engines of the train as it stopped

at the station by the oil field. Kenny stepped out, his black shoes reflecting the midday sun. His narrowed eyes scanned the area and the rigs that pumped oil out of the ground. He had never known this place existed, not until recently.

"Mr. Michaels?" A man in average attire approached Kenny with his hand outstretched.

"Yes," said Kenny with an air of authority and arrogance.

"My name is Lawson. I am here to be your guide. If you need anything, let me know."

Kenny shook the man's outstretched hand and let it drop. "Right now, I require some rest," Kenny eyed the arid landscape, "and some water."

"Right away, sir." Lawson picked up Kenny's bags and led him away. They entered a small building with a single bed on one end and a small sink and toilet on another. "These are your accommodations, sir. I apologize for not being able to get you something better. Unfortunately, we are very cut off from civilization. But there is running water and an air conditioning unit."

"It will do," said Kenny as he looked around the meager room. Already, he missed the mansion his father lived on.

"I will have food brought to you right away. I know you must be tired from your long trip."

"No," said Kenny. "I wish to see what the trouble is with the rail line."

"Yes, sir."

Lawson deposited the bags on the floor. He snatched a hard hat from the table in the middle of the room and handed it to Kenny. "If you'll follow me, sir."

Kenny put on the hat and followed Lawson outside.

They strolled past the oil rigs. Many of the workers looked up momentarily from their duties to observe him and his tailored suit. Officers quickly made them resume their work.

"These rigs, sir, are what provide for the energy in Dystopia," said Lawson."

"What about those wind turbines?" asked Kenny, pointing to a hill with a whole line of them.

"Mostly for show," replied Lawson. "They provide some power, but not reliably. Besides, we need oil to keep them running; otherwise, they won't turn on and the gears grind. The rail line in question is right here."

Lawson stopped on a small rise. He pointed down into the valley where men with no shirts labored steadily. Sweat gleamed off their backs as they lugged railroad ties and giant spikes.

Kenny watched the proceedings dispassionately. "They appear to be making progress. What seems to be the problem?"

"The steel rails are rusted through," said Lawson. "President Klens has refused to give us updated materials to rebuild the line, yet she expects us to deliver the resources on time."

Kenny gave Lawson a piercing look for his crack about the president. As the man cringed underneath his gaze, he relaxed it. It's not his fault. "Very well," said Kenny. "Is there a phone I can use?"

"We have satellite communications in the control tower."

"Take me to it. I will call my father and see to it that all necessary materials are sent."

"Thank you, sir." Lawson bowed and led Kenny to the control tower.

They hiked up the winding staircase to the box-like building at the top. Kenny stepped into the small space with giant windows for walls. The moment he stepped through the door, people looked up from their tasks. Even officers paused. A part of Kenny relished this kind of power, the power to literally stop people in their tracks.

"Patch me through to my father," he said.

A woman punched a few keys on her keyboard before handing him a headset with a microphone.

"First Councilman here."

"Father," said Kenny.

"Kenny, my boy. You have a comfortable trip?"

"Yes, father, but I am calling on business," said Kenny.

"Straight to work. Perfect."

"We need new and updated steel rails and ties for the freight line to be properly repaired."

"But President Klens has…"

"I am perfectly aware of her orders," said Kenny, "but if she wishes to get the oil from here to where she is, then she must listen to reason."

"Kenny…"

"You sent me here to repair the line and that is what I intend to do. Send me the materials I need and I will have this repaired within a month's time."

"That quick?"

Kenny would do it that quickly, determined as he was to not spend a minute longer in this desolate place.

"Very well, I will send you what you need."

"And the president?"

"I will deal with her."

"Thank you, father." Kenny broke the connection and turned to Lawson. "The new rails and ties will be here in a couple of days. See to it that everything is prepared for laying the new line."

"Yes, sir." Lawson ran off.

Kenny strode from the control room. He watched as men toiled over the rigs under the lash of the officers. Still confused about why his father sent him there, he formulated a plan for how best to get the repairs on the railroad done quickly. Kenny rubbed his shoulder. Ever since he left home, it had itched every so often. Must be the dry climate, he thought.

CHAPTER

ELEVEN

Dana cinched the strap to her saddle bag as she made her last-minute preparations.

"Almost ready?" Malcolm asked.

"Yes," said Dana to the leader of the trading caravan. She mounted her horse and rode up beside Sampson, who was determined to stay near her.

"You two take care of yourselves," said Minny as she waved to them.

"Ah, woman, quit nagging," Sampson said affectionately.

They rode through the back country all morning in a single line with their horses, wagons, and one goat. The caravan never used motorized vehicles.

"They get stuck and gasoline is unreliable," Malcolm had told Dana when she asked about it.

She didn't mind the horses. In some ways, she liked them better than cars. She patted Poboy between the ears.

Despite the sun shining, a definite chill hung in the air. Many within the caravan had commented that winter would come early that year. Dana thought it was already there. *Or, perhaps, it hits Dystopia before anywhere else.* She followed along with the members of the trading caravan, many of whom ignored her. They weren't trying to be rude, they just didn't have much to say.

"How're ya doing?" asked Sampson.

Dana smiled at him. "Fine. You've done this sort of thing before, haven't you?"

"I was a trader once, when I was about your age."

"What made you stop?" asked Dana.

"Minny," replied Sampson, "and the fact that I always wanted to own my own land. I believe it's every man's right to own his own land and life."

Dana stared straight ahead, pondering his words.

"What about you?" asked Sampson. "What do you believe?"

"I… I don't know," said Dana.

"You must believe in something."

"What do you mean?"

"No man can go through life without any sort of conviction," said Sampson. "You have to believe in something. Otherwise, you will fall for everything."

"What do you believe in?"

"I believe that a man's life is his own. No human being was meant to be a slave, but many live like one. They allow their lives to be dictated, and many don't realize it.

"I believe that people have the right to work for what they want and to keep the fruit of that labor. What you earn in life is yours to keep and belongs to no one else."

"What about the common good?" asked Dana. She thought back to what she had always been taught.

"What about it?"

"Well, shouldn't people who are able help others?"

"Only if that is their choice," said Sampson, "There has been a lot of harm done in the name of the common good."

"Back home, I was taught that such sentiment was selfishness."

"It isn't selfish to want to keep the money you earn, Dana. It is selfish to want to take what another has because you think he doesn't deserve it."

"What about charity?"

"Charity is not charity when it is forced. If you wish to give your own things away, then by all means, do so. But charity must come from your heart. It must be your decision."

"No one has ever said such things to me before."

"You asked me what I believe and I told you. You, Dana, will need to figure out for yourself what you will believe in. What principles will you adhere to? Make sure you choose wisely because they will dictate the course of your life. And there are always consequences to your decisions."

Tall structures in the distance grabbed Dana's attention. She turned to Sampson. "What are those?"

Sampson stared at the structures for a moment. "Not sure," he said.

"Maybe we should take a closer look," suggested Dana.

Sampson grunted.

"It's the only way to find out what they are," said Dana.

Sampson whistled at Malcolm and pointed at the spindly towers. Malcolm nodded in affirmation. Steering their horses, they galloped toward the towers for a closer look. Dana kept her eyes fixed on them, her mind racing with the possibilities. After a few hours, they had finally reached them. Sampson halted his horse and motioned for her to do the same.

Dana followed his movements. She dismounted and tied Poboy to a log lying on the ground.

"We will wait here," said Malcolm, "while you two go inspect."

Crawling over the sand, Dana and Sampson inched their way up a small, round hill. Brush and sticks snagged her jacket. Each time, Dana tugged herself free, careful to not make too much noise. Voices reached her ears. The closer they came, the louder the voices. Peeking over the sandy hill, Dana gasped at what she saw. The Dystopian flag whipped in the wind from a lonely pole in the middle of the field. Officers patrolled the outer area, their guns raised and ready for action. She watched as the giant structures moved like dumbwaiters, in fluid up and down strokes.

"What is all this?" she asked.

"Oil rigs," said Sampson. "I haven't seen one in a long time. There used to be a time when these things were all over the place, but they were destroyed."

Dana studied the oil rigs as they pumped the black liquid from the ground. "I never knew they had these here."

"I'm not surprised," said Sampson. "Looks like your government has had these awhile and intends on keeping it a secret."

Dana wanted a closer look. She scooted from her hiding place and crept to the bottom of the hill, hiding behind equipment. Officers strolled by, unaware of her presence. Carefully, Dana watched as men worked on the oil rigs. She figured they had been undesirables sent there to labor until they died.

"Dana," hissed Sampson as he came up behind her. "What are you doing?"

Before Dana could answer, Sampson shoved her against the equipment, pointing at a camera as it scanned the area. "We need to leave, now."

Dana agreed.

Shouts and yells rose up around her. Dana peeked around the equipment. Men darted about as a plume of oil shot from the ground. Black liquid rained down upon the workers as they rushed about to stem the flow. Dana watched as they grabbed a cap for the wellhead and placed it on the opening. Three men turned a giant wrench as they sealed it. Oil covered the ground once the commotion had ceased.

"Dana." Sampson pulled her away.

They raced up the hill, their feet sliding on the sand before leaping over it, clinging to the ground and hoping no one saw them. Cautiously, Sampson peeked down into the oil field. Officers and workers busied themselves with the rigs, completely unaware of the two spies.

Quickly, Sampson and Dana ran back to where Malcolm and the others waited. They mounted their horses and sped off, Dana's mind racing with questions about the oil field.

When night fell, they stopped and set up tents and a fire. Dana watched as they worked swiftly, having done this so many times before. One man handed her a small container with some sort of red paste in it. He motioned for her to try some. Gingerly, she scooped a little bit onto her finger and tasted it. Instantly, her mouth felt as though it were on fire. Sweat formed on her face as her mouth became an inferno.

Many of the traders laughed to themselves. Dana grabbed her canteen of water and took a big swig from it. It made it worse. She stuck her tongue out and waved air at it to cool it off. More laughter erupted from the men.

Suddenly, Malcolm appeared. He scolded the men in a language she didn't know before handing her some goat's milk and flat bread. "Eat these," he said.

Dana did. She chugged the milk and chewed on the bread. Gradually, the fire in her mouth dissipated.

"I apologize for my men," said Malcolm, looking at her with eyes lined from having spent all his life in the sand and the sun. "They think it is funny to initiate new members with the spice paste. It is a dish made from the smallest peppers. But the smaller the pepper, the hotter it is."

Dana watched Malcolm with tears in her eyes from the spices. "It's fine," she said, though it came out funny with her numb tongue.

"You just keep chewing the bread and drinking the milk," said Malcolm. "It will clear up soon."

Dana did as ordered, glad to have some relief for her mouth. She vowed never to eat unidentified food again.

"How do you navigate through here?" asked Dana as she looked up at the many stars in the sky. She had never seen so many. The black sky seemed to come alive with them.

"It's not too difficult," said Malcolm. "That there is the North Star, Polaris. If you can find it, then you will have no trouble knowing where you are."

"But what about during the day when you cannot see the stars?" asked Dana.

"Well, the sun always rises in the east, sets in the west,

and spends most of its time in the southern sky," replied Malcolm. "Every morning and evening, Venus appears."

Dana listened intently as Malcolm described how he navigated using the stars and the sun. She wished she had had such knowledge earlier.

"And as long as you know where your destination is," continued Malcolm, "then you will never get lost."

"How long have you traveled the desert?"

"My whole life. My father did it before me and my grandfather did it before him. One day, my son will do the same." He glanced at a teenage boy who laughed and joked with the others.

"What if he wants to do something else?" asked Dana.

Malcolm turned to her. "He has never shown any desire to. If he had, he would have left long ago. No man stays on the desert if they do not wish to."

"How did this place become so barren?" asked Dana.

"No one really knows," said Malcolm. "Stories abound, but the truth remains hidden. But it will not always be this way."

"How do you know?"

"Look." Malcolm pointed to a small pool of water and bits of greenery that blossomed there. "That was not there the last time I came through here."

Dana touched the cool water, amazed that even in a place so bereft of living things, life was to be found.

"When you have finished eating," said Malcolm, "you should sleep. We should reach the ruined city by midday tomorrow."

Dana stretched out. She glanced over at Sampson, who lay on his back with his hat over his face snoring. *That man could sleep through anything.* Eventually, Dana drifted off.

By afternoon the next day, the caravan came to the ruined city, the same city Dana had entered when she wandered lost in the desert. She held lightly to the reins, looking upon the ruins with a new perspective. They didn't seem so barren like before.

"We will split up," said Malcolm. "Find what you can and meet back here within the hour. Sampson, you stay with Dana."

Sampson nodded, though Dana figured he would have stayed with her anyway. Together, they steered their horses to a more remote area of the city.

"This looks like a good place to find some stuff," said Sampson.

Dana hopped off Poboy and tied him to a post. She wandered into what appeared to have been a house at some point. Her foot crunched on some glass. Curious, she reached down and picked up a faded photograph. The frame had protected it until she had broken it. A man stood smiling as he hugged his wife and children. Dana's heart ached a bit as she remembered her parents and the end they had met. She longed for her family. Carefully, she put the picture on a cluttered table.

Some wiring hung from the ceiling. Dana tugged at it a bit. It pulled easily. Remembering that wiring was a prized commodity, she yanked on it some more until it came free. Dana coiled it up and stuffed it in her bag.

She spotted a refrigerator that seemed to be in good condition. "Sampson," she called, "could someone use this?"

Sampson hurried in. He studied the appliance, inspecting the coils on the back. "Seems to be in fair condition. I think someone will find a use for it."

He pulled it from the wall and scooted it outside.

Together, he and Dana heaved it into a wagon. Sampson tied it down with some rope. "There. That ought to fetch a good price." The man looked up at the sun. "We ought to get back."

Dana followed after him, but paused momentarily. Something green had caught her attention. She strode over to it and picked it up. The frayed cover of a book about the life of Patrick Henry filled her hands. Carefully, Dana inspected the pages. They seemed intact.

"Dana!"

She pocketed the book and hurried after Sampson.

Malcolm was pleased at their find when they met up with the rest of the group. Many of the guys had found similar items to be sold in neighboring towns.

A scuffling sound echoed behind them. They all whirled around, pulling out their guns.

"Don't shoot," said a swarthy man as he crawled out of a small hole. "Don't shoot. I come peaceably."

Dana recognized him immediately as one of the bandits that had attacked her.

"Who are you?" demanded Sampson.

"Ailes," said the man. "Please, don't shoot." The man noticed Dana for the first time. "Hey, you're that whore who knocked my friends and me unconscious."

He charged her. Dana stepped back. Malcolm and his men immediately grabbed him and subdued the man.

"My mistake," he said. "Really."

"Is he one of the guys that attacked you?" asked Sampson.

"Yes," said Dana. "But there were three others."

"Where are your friends?" asked Sampson.

"They left me," whined Ailes. "They blamed me for her getting away."

"And just what were you planning to do with her?"

Ailes struggled internally between telling Sampson the truth or keeping his mouth shut. "Nothing. Nothing. We just wanted company."

"Yeah, I know what you wanted." Sampson punched the man in the face. "That's for kidnapping her. And this"—he punched the man again—"is for preying upon other innocent folk."

Dana thought his actions were a bit harsh, but she kept her mouth shut. She knew that the wasteland had a separate set of rules and Sampson's mannerisms told her that he had had dealings with bandits before.

"You asshole," yelled the man. "I'll get even with you for this."

"Go on, get out of here," said Sampson, shoving the man away.

"You'll regret this," said Ailes.

"Yeah. Yeah." Sampson fired a couple of shots at the man's feet. "Get, before I change my mind."

Ailes darted off.

"You don't approve," said Sampson to Dana when he noticed the look on her face.

"It seems a bit harsh," she said.

"Maybe so," replied Sampson, "but all of us here have had encounters with men like him. One such scum wandered into town once. He passed himself off as a trader. Later, I learned who he truly was when he raped my daughter. A few weeks later, she killed herself from the shame. Now, that scum may not have been the one to do it, but he's no different from the rest."

"Time to leave," said Malcolm.

Everyone packed their items and headed off. Dana followed, her mind racing with the new information she had learned about her friend. It seemed to Dana that everyone had a tragic story.

"Don't mind him," said Malcolm. "It's a painful part of his past that will never heal. But what he did today was quite merciful."

"What do you mean?" asked Dana.

"When Sampson's daughter died, he went crazy. He saddled his horse, grabbed his shotgun, and hunted down every bandit and thief he could find until he came upon the one that harmed his daughter."

"What did he do to the man?"

"Do you really need to ask?"

Dana guessed what had happened. "What changed him?"

"Well, Minny mostly," answered Malcolm, "and the realization that killing the guy would never bring his daughter back. Oh, I'm not saying that he didn't get what he deserved. But Sampson realized what only the very wise know, that revenge never makes the pain go away."

"Oh."

"Course, one thing you need to realize if you are going to live here is that this place is full of thieves like Ailes. They care nothing for others. Only their desires matter to them. When you meet one, you have only two choices. Either they die, or you.

"But that is enough serious talk for today. We managed to gather enough items to travel to the next town for bartering. Once we have finished there, we will head back to Libre."

Dana smiled. She looked forward to auctioning off her find.

"How do you like the life of a trader?" asked Malcolm.

"It's freeing," said Dana. "I get to choose my own ends."

The horses' hooves clopped on the ground as the caravan entered the neighboring town of Rowles. They pushed the wagons to the town square. Instantly, people dropped what they were doing and gathered around with excitement. Days that the traders arrived were always days of anticipation.

Malcolm motioned where to park the wagons. His men pulled them into a single line and ripped off the coverings.

Dana watched as people approached with their coins or items they wished to trade. She had never seen such a thing before. Casually, people perused through the items in the wagons, picking what they wanted. Afterward, they walked up to one of the traders and haggled over the price.

"How much?" asked a man holding up the wire Dana had procured.

"Uh," Dana was unsure of what to say. "Fifty coins."

"Fifty, that's more than I've got."

Dana had never negotiated the price of something before. She looked at the wheelbarrow the man had. One item caught her interest. "I'll take that gun and its belt for the wire."

The man looked at the six-shooter. It was more of an antique.

"And any ammunition that goes with it."

"Done."

Dana took the gun, its holster, and bullets. She handed the coiled wire over to a grateful man who thought he had just outwitted her. Dana let him think he had won. She had never owned a weapon before and wanted one, considering the dangers of her new home.

She turned while fingering her new purchase. A man inspected the refrigerator that she had found earlier. "May I help you?"

"Does this thing work?" asked the man.

"I think so," replied Dana.

"You think so?"

"I haven't tested it yet."

The frown on the man's face told her that he didn't approve. "I'll give you 12 coins for it."

Dana pursed her lips. It was not a fair offer and the man knew it. "No deal."

"I'm being more than generous," said the man.

"No, you're not. You're trying to cheat me."

"I won't offer more."

"I won't sell for less than 100."

The man kicked at the dirt and stormed away, infuriated that he had failed to con Dana out of such a treasure.

"He's always looking for a steal," said a bony woman with an infant on her hip. "I could really use that."

Dana studied the young mother. Pity filled her. Noticing the binoculars around the woman's neck, she decided to make an offer. "Nice binoculars."

"Oh," the woman touched them with a slight smile, "they were my late husband's. Don't know why I carry them around."

"Sorry," said Dana. "Uh…"

"You know," said the woman, taking the binoculars off and handing them to Dana. "I don't need them. Here, for the fridge."

Dana took the field glasses. "How will you…"

"I'll send someone by this evening for it." The woman left.

By sunset, the crowd faded and the traders packed their wares. Dana eyed the wagons, remarking at the new items within them and how most of the old stuff had disappeared.

"So how did you like you first real market day?" asked Malcolm.

"It was good." Dana showed him the weapon.

Raising an eyebrow, Malcolm seemed surprised. "That is a real beauty. You best keep it close."

He gave the signal, and his men closed up the wagons. After a hearty meal in the local eatery, Dana looked forward to some sleep. Today was perfect, she thought to herself, nothing could upset my life here.

CHAPTER TWELVE

Kenny stood upon the flat car watching as the workers repaired the railroad. The new steel rails gleamed in the sunlight. He glanced out at the sandy expanse. *What a miserable place.* Since the day Kenny arrived, he had counted down the days to when he could go home.

"We are ready to test it," said one of the workers.

"Very well," said Kenny.

"Do you wish to move to the closed car?"

"No," replied Kenny. "I will remain on the flatcar with you. I can see everything much better this way."

"Yes, sir."

The man hollered to the engineer to start up the train. "Start the engine!"

The engine roared to life. Gradually, the train moved forward, picking up speed as it went. Kenny watched dispassionately as it moved toward the new track. The workers nervously waited to see if their repairs would hold. Every time he looked at one of them, they jumped nervously. Such is the way of things, thought Kenny.

The train sped up even more. A huge lurch alerted him that something was terribly wrong. "What was that?" he asked.

"Not sure," said the worker.

The train jumped a second time. This time, everyone panicked.

"Pull the brake," yelled the worker next to Kenny.

Someone yanked on the lever. It snapped and the train continued to race down the tracks. A sinking feeling filled Kenny as he realized they weren't slowing down.

Dana looked down the hill as the trading caravan rode along the rail. They had seen the workers on the tracks and decided to take another way back to Libre, not wanting to alert them to their presence. The squealing wheels of the train alerted her to their distress. Stopping, she pulled out her binoculars and peered through them.

Kenny stood on one of the cars. Dana nearly dropped the binoculars in shock. What was he doing here? She focused them again and studied the movement of the train as it gathered more speed. Instantly, she realized that it was a runaway train.

Dana looked further ahead. One of the rails had come undone and off the railroad ties. Dana knew that if the train hit that area, it would derail and kill everyone aboard.

"What is it?" asked Sampson.

Dana handed him the binoculars. He looked through them. "They don't have a prayer."

Dana took back the binoculars, taking one more glance at Kenny as he and the others tried to stop the train. The car jerked, knocking one man off. For a fleeting second, she considered just letting him suffer his fate. Quickly, she pushed the thought away.

"We have to help them," she said.

"How? It's too dangerous."

"We have to do something."

"Dana…"

Dana cracked the reins of her horse, speeding off down the hillside toward the train. She had no plan, other than to somehow pull Kenny off the flatcar before the train derailed.

Poboy snorted heavily as she raced for the speeding train. Clouds of dust billowed behind her. Shouts and yells filtered through the commotion, but Dana ignored them. She couldn't just let a friend die. Her conscience would not allow it.

Once on the bottom, Dana steered Poboy in the same direction as the train. She felt the animal's muscles strain under the effort. Pushing onward, she sped up until she reached the flat car.

"Kenny!" yelled Dana.

Kenny looked over. "Dana?" He stared at her stupidly as though he saw a ghost. "What are you doing here?"

"No time! Take my hand."

The train lurched again, causing another man to lose his balance and tumble over. Dana refused to focus on it. Her mind lay only with saving Kenny, and the others if possible.

"Take my hand!" she shouted again over the thundering wheels.

Carefully, Kenny hung onto a guardrail and reached out.

He brushed fingers with Dana. She steered her horse a little closer, but didn't dare to go further.

"Jump!" yelled Dana.

"I can't!"

Dana glanced ahead. They were too close to the missing section of the track.

"You have to jump!" she shouted again.

Kenny looked at the ground as it sped past. "This is impossible!"

"Kenny, you spineless—Jump!"

A man came up behind Kenny. He noted the missing track as well. Taking one glance at Dana, they locked eyes a moment. Suddenly, the man pushed Kenny off the car and towards Dana's outstretched hand.

Dana and Kenny grasped arms. She heaved him onto her horse and steered it away from the train just as it hit the missing rail. Instantly, the train leapt off the tracks, turning over. Cars separated as debris flew everywhere. Not daring to look back, Dana kicked Poboy and galloped away from there.

Once she determined they were a safe distance away, she slowed. Turning back around, she and Kenny watched as the train scattered over the desert like a tumbled stack of matchsticks. Clouds of sand formed with each new impact.

"What the hell were you thinking?" demanded Sampson as he rode up with the others.

"I wasn't," admitted Dana.

"Well that is pretty evident. You… idiotic… of all the things…" Sampson didn't finish his statement. He didn't need to. Dana knew what he thought.

"Here," Malcolm handed Kenny a canister of water. Unsure of the people before him, Kenny took it, glad to have a drink. His hands shook so badly that Dana had to help him hold the canteen.

"Sorry," Dana apologized to Sampson again. "I just reacted."

"Yeah, well people tend to do that. The heroes are the ones lucky enough to survive their rash decisions."

Dana glanced at her saddle.

"Don't ever do that again," said Sampson.

"Yes, Sampson."

"Boy, you will ride with Malcolm," said Sampson to Kenny.

Kenny didn't argue. He switched horses, still wondering about the trustworthiness of these people.

"Well, we got a ways to go before we reach town," said Sampson, "Best get going."

Night fell before they reached Libre, so Malcolm had them set up camp. His men made a small fire and posted lookouts. Kenny just watched as everyone went about their business oblivious to his presence.

One of the men showed up with a couple of rabbits he had just caught. Dana took one, grabbed her knife, and set about skinning it. Minny had taught her how. After doing it several times, it no longer disgusted her. Her hunger always overrode her sentiments.

"Ugh," said Kenny as he watched.

"What?" asked Dana as she sliced off bits of meat and placed them on the fire.

"What you're doing," Kenny replied.

Dana didn't understand his statement.

"Where do you think your food comes from?" asked Sampson as he walked by.

Kenny glared at him with dislike. He didn't like being talked down to. "I don't like him."

"Who?" asked Dana. "Sampson? He's a good man."

"I'm the First Councilman's son and he treats me like everyone else."

"Because out here, nobody cares about your parentage." Dana handed him some of the cooked rabbit.

Kenny looked at it doubtfully.

"I'm sorry if we can't offer you more luxurious accommodations," said Dana without sympathy, "but that's all we have to eat out here. If you're hungry, just bite and chew."

Kenny's grumbling stomach overrode his sensibilities. He nibbled on the rabbit meat, surprised that it didn't taste that bad. "Dana? How'd you end up out here?"

"Complete accident," replied Dana. "I hopped off the train I was on and ended up wandering around here lost before I ran into Sampson. He and his wife took me in."

"I thought you were dead."

"Sorry to disappoint." Dana sat next to him with her supper. She ate big chunks and drank from her canteen with no shred of ladylike grace.

"Why did you save me?" asked Kenny. The question had gnawed at him all afternoon.

Dana stopped eating and looked at him. "Because you're my friend."

Her matter-of-fact tone startled Kenny. He had expected her to hold a grudge after what his father had done. "I didn't know," he said, "I didn't know about your parents."

"I know." Dana rested a reassuring hand on his.

Kenny noticed a book sticking out of Dana's pack. He

pulled it out and read the cover as the firelight danced on it. "What's this?"

"A book," said Dana.

"Yes, but its contraband."

"Not out here. I found it and plan on reading it."

"But Patrick Henry was a bigoted, white racist who only cared about himself."

Dana snatched the book from him. "You're just repeating what you have always been told. I am going to read this book and form my own opinion. And not you or anyone else is going to force me to do otherwise."

"Dana, I would never force you to do anything," said Kenny.

"Sometimes I wonder about you, Kenny. In so many ways, you are like your father, but in other ways, you are different. I just wonder what it is you will choose to be."

"Dana…"

"You should finish eating and get some sleep. We have an early start in the morning."

Dana stood up and walked over to Poboy. Kenny watched as she petted his muzzle while cooing to him. She nuzzled into the horse's fur before settling down for the night. Kenny didn't understand Dana's newfound independence, or why she loved that horse. It's just a filthy animal, he thought. He rolled onto his side and drifted to sleep, despite the pockets of conversation among the traders that lasted well into the night.

CHAPTER

THIRTEEN

Kenny woke up with a sore arm. He glanced at it, noticing the bloodied rag tied around it. "What the…"

"I cut out your chip," said Dana, "while you slept."

"You drugged me."

"So you wouldn't feel the pain. Would you rather I hadn't?"

"You had no right."

"Perhaps not, but I won't risk your father being able to use it to track you and me."

"But—how am I to get back home?"

Dana eyed her friend. "If you really wish to return, you know where the tracks are. Just follow them and eventually you will reenter Dystopia."

"By myself?"

"You really are helpless," said Dana. She finished securing the bags to her horse. "Kenny, I don't have time to argue with you. You can either find your own way back home, or quit complaining and come with us. The choice is yours."

Dana mounted Poboy and galloped off.

The trading caravan entered town by early evening. People gathered around like they did in the previous place. Many waited impatiently to buy and sell goods, but Malcolm never liked doing business at night.

"Please, all of you," he addressed the crowd, "we are tired from our long journey. We will conduct business in the morning."

A few moans escaped their mouths as disappointment enveloped them. Slowly, they dispersed, vowing to return in the morning.

"We should get something to eat," said Sampson.

He led Dana and Kenny to Betsy's diner. Malcolm and his crew joined them.

"Well, well, well, if it isn't the girl who ran out on me to wander in the wilderness," greeted Betsy in her usual crass manner.

"Evening, Betsy," said Sampson. "We are all famished and would like your special."

"I don't offer anything for free," said Betsy.

Sampson laughed. "Put it on my tab."

"I don't do tabs."

"You do for me. Have I ever not paid you?"

Betsy huffed and went back into the kitchen.

"She likes to huff and puff, but she really is soft at heart," said Sampson.

"What is this place?" asked Kenny.

"Home," said Dana. "My new home."

"What do you mean? You're not coming back to Dystopia?"

"Why would I, Kenny? I can't go back there. You know that."

"You wouldn't be in this position if you hadn't made that speech during your honor ceremony."

"Honor ceremony?" Dana eyed her friend. "That ceremony was not made to honor me. It was staged to turn me into a hero before your father and Colonel Fernau had me killed."

"My father would never…"

"He lied about my parents. Do you think they would actually tell the truth about me? And while we're at it, why were you on the railroad?"

"My father wanted me to oversee the railroad repairs."

"That doesn't make sense," said Dana. "Usually, they send a low ranking officer, not the son of the First Councilman."

"What are you implying?" asked Kenny.

"It's just strange," said Dana.

Betsy plopped two plates on the table, each containing steak, eggs, buttered toast, and an apple. Kenny stared at his plate. "These are all contraband items," he said.

"Like that ever stopped you from eating them before," said Dana digging into her food.

"Well, yes, but…" Kenny's voice trailed off.

"I suggest you eat," said Dana.

"But for the good of our nation…"

"Kenny, that nonsense means nothing here," said Dana. "You have food before you now. You best eat it because you might not have anything to eat tomorrow."

Kenny glared at Dana. He didn't like being scolded. No one ever told him what to do, except for his father. Even many officers refused to challenge him because of his father's station.

"Well, you two," said Sampson joining them, "I hope you like your supper. Betsy always makes the best steak."

Sampson noticed that Kenny hadn't touched his food. "Well, eat up, son, you've got a long day tomorrow."

"What do you mean?" asked Kenny.

"Well, if you're going to stay here, you need to find a way to earn a living. Got any skills?"

Kenny looked at his plate.

"He can start here," said Dana.

"Work here?" said Kenny. "In this dump?"

"It's where I started," said Dana. "Sorry, Kenny, but your father isn't here to get you a cushy job."

Sampson watched their exchange with interest. "Well, you can start working in the stables. Mr. Callors always needs help keeping it clean. It's a good place to start until you work your way up."

"What do you mean?" asked Kenny.

"I started working here," said Dana. "Then, when I figured out that I wanted to join the traders, I saved my money and bought a horse and supplies."

"Without a license?" Kenny was aghast that Dana would do such a thing.

"Why would she need a license?" asked Sampson.

"In Dystopia, we need a permit to do anything. Including to blow our nose," mumbled Dana.

"That's not true," said Kenny, sharply.

"You're right," replied Dana. "If you are from a privileged family, or your parents write the rules, then you can do anything without suffering the consequences.

"Getting your hands dirty isn't going to kill you, Kenny. If you're frugal, you can save enough money to start your own business."

"Is that your plan?" asked Kenny.

"Yes," replied Dana. "I plan to travel with the traders until I learn the area and how to acquire things people need. Then I will bring them back here and sell them."

"That's a good plan," said Sampson. "However, the cold months are coming and Malcolm and his crew always go south for the winter. Some of the storms get pretty bad."

"Yes, Malcolm told me that," said Dana. "However, Minny said that she could use help canning the harvested fruit from your fields. I figured if we had enough, we'd sell the extras, and Betsy agreed to let me work here."

"You two ladies have been conspiring against me," joked Sampson.

"So, anyone can start a shop here?" said Kenny.

"If they have a mind to and the willingness to work at it," replied Sampson.

"But what if they fail?"

"That is always a risk."

"But, shouldn't there be measures in place to ensure the fair opportunity for every person to succeed?" asked Kenny.

"We have one," said Sampson, "It's the people. If you have something they want to buy, you'll succeed. If you don't, you close up shop.

"Now, I suggest you finish eating. It's getting late. Dana, I'll see you back at the farm. And there's a room for you as well, Kenny, if you wish."

Sampson left them while Kenny continued to pick at his greasy plate.

CHAPTER

FOURTEEN

President Klens admired herself in the vanity mirror. She straightened her sapphire necklace and earrings, relishing the way they set off her purple blouse and tanned skin tone. *Oh, those poor wretches. They work so hard so that I might live comfortably.* President Klens chuckled inwardly. It always amused her how many of the masses thought she actually cared about them.

"Madam President," said Williams, "they are ready for you."

"Thank you, Williams."

President Klens rose from her chair and walked over to the stage entrance for the televised program. She loved coming onto these shows. Of course, they had all been approved by her in the first place, and the hosts knew to be friendly. Not that they would have dared to be otherwise. They each believed in her definition of equality and feared the consequences of disagreeing.

"And now, let me introduce to you, our honored guest for the evening, President Klens," said the show host, Halloway.

Cheers and applause went up from the studio audience. The band played triumphant music, welcoming the president as she walked out on the stage smiling and waving. Oh, what easily entertained fools, she thought.

"President Klens," greeted Halloway. "It is so nice to see you again on my show."

"And I always enjoy being here, Halloway."

The two took their seats.

"That is a lovely outfit," said Halloway. "Many say that your fashion sense is remarkable and I must agree."

"Thank you. I do try to look presentable."

"As you know, many of our audience always have questions for you."

"I always enjoy answering them."

"I have a few of them here." Halloway took out some cue cards. "Ah, Ginny here wants to know what your favorite book is."

"Ginny? Where is Ginny? Oh, hello, Ginny. Well, there are so many books, and I am a voracious reader, but there is one that stands out, Clarkson's *Learning to Live as One*.

"It is a remarkable book which points out the very values we have created for our society: equality, fairness, openness, and the welfare of the common good. These are principles I have always tried to live by, and I think that they have proven fruitful for all of us.

"As you are all aware, there are some selfish individuals who would rather put their wants above everyone else. This we cannot allow."

"This brings us to an interesting topic," said Halloway. "As you know, there are those who insist that we are not free in this society and openly demand the abolition of many of our boards, such as the Career Assignment Board. How would you respond to them?"

President Klens' face tightened a bit. She had not expected this question. In fact, it was not in the script she had received earlier. As she scanned the faces of the live audience and knew the cameras rolled with each passing second, she smiled.

"Well, Mr. Halloway, I think we both know that they are not only lying, but they are also disgruntled individuals who are jealous of what we have achieved.

"We have achieved true equality in Dystopia. Each person works according to their abilities in the job that fits them best. By assigning employment, we have ensured that every citizen has a job. Everyone is equal, and no one is able to rise above another.

"Those with a flair for leading and making policies are the ministry. Those with an aptitude for law enforcement become the officers. While those whose physical strength best suits them for manual labor work in the various facilities and plants. No one is above another as we all—by working together—form a cohesive society.

"We are a collective family where every member has a role to play. Our Career Assignment Board, like all of the boards, helps each individual find and fulfill their role. And as you will notice, there is no unemployment."

"That is a valid point that I think the naysayers routinely forget," said Halloway,

"No one in our society has to worry about looking for work because everyone has a job."

"Indeed," said Halloway. "Next question: do you like whole wheat or multigrain bread?"

President Klens laughed. "I prefer whole wheat, of course."

"Yes, it's healthier for you. Well, on to the next. This one comes from Billy, the boy in the front row."

Billy waved at the two on the stage with a gleeful expression.

"Billy wants to know what your favorite subject in school was."

"Well, Billy, I loved school when I was your age, but I must say that my favorite subject was physical education class," said President Klens as her chin jiggled. "I enjoy exercise and always loved being able to jog around the track. Do you like to run, Billy?"

Billy's head nodded enthusiastically.

"Good. It keeps you fit and healthy."

"I must say that my favorite part about physical education," laughed Halloway, "was watching the girls in their running shorts."

President Klens chuckled. "Well, we can't all enjoy that, can we?"

"No, I suppose not," said Halloway. "This next question is from me. I promised to ask a serious question. Do you prefer raisins or cranberries as an afternoon snack?"

"Well, I like both," guffawed President Klens. "That was a serious question?"

Halloway laughed before his tone grew more serious. "As you know, there has been an energy crisis in our country. Many homes in the northern sectors have no heating and winter is almost here."

"Yes, and I lay awake every night wondering how we can come together to fix the problem."

"Well, some in our audience would like to know how you plan to solve our limited energy resources."

"As many of you already know, oil and coal are severely limited resources, and we cannot depend upon foreign imports as the world is in complete disarray. Something Dystopia has managed to avoid, I might add. We have tried a variety of other technologies which do work, but not effectively. So, as of yesterday, I proposed that we look into geothermal energy sources. What could be more environmentally friendly and efficient than to use the earth's energy to suit our needs?"

Applause rose up.

"I will personally make sure that advancements in geothermal technology are made so that no citizen is without heat in the winter and cooling in the summer."

More applause.

"That is quite a promise," said Halloway, "and I am sure you will fulfill it. As always, you do have our best interests in mind."

"Not a day goes by where I don't think about it."

"Well, that is all the time we have for tonight. Thank you, President Klens, for taking time out of your busy schedule to meet with us here."

"As always, it is a pleasure."

President Klens and Halloway shook hands before parting.

An employee at the television station handed President Klens a glass of water as she walked backstage.

"Thank you, dear. Those stage lights always make me

thirsty," said the president as she took a swig. "Where is my lemon? I never drink water without a lemon." She handed the glass back to the frightened employee.

"Incompetent people," muttered President Klens.

"That was a wonderful show," said Williams. "It should keep the public appeased despite the resistance's efforts to disrupt things."

"One can only hope."

"Madam President," said Williams, "didn't your grandfather have the only known scientists with advanced knowledge of utilizing geothermal energy executed?"

"What of it?" asked President Klens with little concern.

"How do you propose to keep your promise on its development?"

"I don't."

"What of those people without adequate electricity?"

President Klens eyed her assistant with cold, calculating eyes. "I guess we won't have to worry about overpopulation."

Chapter Fifteen

Kenny's tired muscles scraped the shovel across the ground as he scooped manure into a bucket. The stench nearly gagged him. *How can people stand to live like this?* The snorting of a horse drew his attention.

"I don't know what you're complaining about," said Kenny, scratching his shoulder.

He had been working in the stables since early morning. Fuming that he had been reduced to manual labor, Kenny lazily scooped more poop into the nearby bucket. Tired, he dropped his shovel and sat down on a barrel.

Mr. Callors walked into the building. "Tired already?" he said when he noticed Kenny taking a break. "You've barely gotten started."

"The work is exhausting," said Kenny.

"Most hard work is," said Mr. Callors. "Now the agreement

was that you would clean out all of this manure before the end of the day. If you don't, I'll have to rethink your wages."

"You can't do that!"

"On the contrary," said Mr. Callors, "I can. You promised to clean this place up in exchange for 300 coins. Now, if the work gets done, I'll pay you what is owed. But if it doesn't, then you will only get paid for the work you actually accomplish."

"That's not fair," said Kenny. "This is hard work. I'm dirty and sweaty. And this place smells. I've never done this work before."

"That much is evident," said Mr. Callors. "Get the job done, or you can leave right now and I'll hire someone else."

"What?"

"You don't have to work here," said Mr. Callors.

"What am I supposed to do if I lose this job?"

Mr. Callors looked at Kenny with no sympathy. "Find something that caters more to your delicate sensibilities."

Angered at being treated like a commoner, Kenny kicked the manure in front of him.

"I see they got you working like a common animal," said Bert as he swaggered in with his bottle of liquor. "Hard work, but little pay. Not fair is it?"

"No, it's not," said Kenny, throwing down the shovel. "Who are you?"

"Bert."

"What are you doing here?" asked Kenny.

"Just come to check on the newest member of our little society," said Bert.

"Oh."

"I heard what you said to Mr. Callors. For a while now,

people like him have been making money off the backs of desperate folk like you."

"What are you saying?"

"Well, with the right person, we could even out the playing field so that all benefit and not just a few."

"Why should I listen to you?" asked Kenny.

"No reason, really," said Bert. "I've been here many years and have never been able to better my circumstances because people like Callors and Sampson don't understand me. They don't understand the nature of addiction. They think that everyone should work hard to get what they want from life. But they don't understand that not everyone is capable of hard work, but they still have needs."

"What do you want from me?"

"You could help those of us who have not been able to rise up. You understand us."

"I don't know," said Kenny.

"Think about it," said Bert.

Dana carefully filled a jar with some preserved apples and sealed it. She had never realized how much work canning involved, but she saw the merit in it.

"That's good," said Minny as she wiped the jar clean.

Dana smiled. "So you do this every year?"

"Yep. It's the best way to stock up food for the winter. Though Sampson has our orchard in a place that is temperature controlled, I still prefer to be prepared."

"Prepared?"

"One year, the electricity failed and we lost most of our crop. That was a lean year."

"Well, it's fixed," said Sampson as he walked inside. He had been on the roof repairing one of their solar panels and their battery source. Karl had developed a technology to draw power from water, but Sampson always liked being prepared. He figured if he had more than one energy source, then when one failed, the other would make up the difference.

"But I need to get a new ionizer," said Sampson.

"I can get it," said Dana. "I have to go to town anyway to see how Kenny is doing. I can stop by the hardware store and pick one up."

Sampson gave Dana the keys to his truck and some money. "You be careful with my truck."

"Oh, please," said Minny. "Sometimes I think you care more about that stupid truck than me."

"Not a scratch," Sampson said to Dana.

"On that rusty old thing?" voiced Minny.

"I promise," said Dana, taking the keys.

Dana hopped into the vehicle and slammed the door shut. She inserted the key into the ignition, glad to be driving a vehicle while not fleeing from a bunch of officers.

She rammed the truck into gear and steered it toward town. The setting sun showered gorgeous orange and red rays over the land. Despite its barrenness, Dana thought the dusk looked beautiful. It had been a long time since she had stopped to admire it.

She arrived into town 10 minutes later and parked near the hardware store. Hopping out of the truck, she noticed Kenny sitting in the bar with Bert and a few others. Curious, she studied them a moment, deciding to ask him about it when she finished her business in the store.

"Evening, Mr. Harris," said Dana to the store owner.

"Why, hello, Dana. And how is the future trader?"

"I'm not a trader yet," replied Dana. "I've only been on one run, and you know I can't go on any more until spring."

"Well, when you do go out with Malcolm again," said Mr. Harris, "try and find me a carbonator, will you?"

"Sure. No problem."

"So, what can I do for you?"

"I need an ionizer. Or actually Sampson needs one."

"Aha," said Mr. Harris, browsing through his stock, "For that weird generator of his, I suspect. Well, it just so happens that I have one. Here."

Mr. Harris placed it in a bag and gave it to Dana. She handed him the money and inspected the merchandise, making certain it was what she needed.

"Thank you, Mr. Harris."

Dana waved and left. She placed the ionizer in the truck and glanced back at the bar window. *Looks like they're breaking up.* Not certain what they were up to, Dana walked over, reaching the door just as Kenny exited with Bert.

"Hey, Dana," greeted Kenny.

"Kenny," said Dana.

"I'll see you later," said Bert, unusually sober.

"What were you doing with him?" asked Dana.

"Bert and I were discussing a few things with some other people."

"What things?"

"Like how it seems that certain people always have money and are at the top of society, while others are at the bottom."

"And what would you know about that, Kenny? You were always at the top back home."

"But we had true equality in Dystopia."

"You really believe that?" Dana looked at her friend concerned. She and Kenny always had their differences, but deep down, she knew he was not a bad person. *Or, has he changed?*

"And why were you talking to Bert?"

"He was explaining to me how things work here. Sampson seems to have a monopoly on the government."

"He was elected mayor and spends most of his time leaving people alone."

"Yeah, but no one ever challenges him."

"But no one is stopping them from doing so," said Dana.

"Well, he has all that property and is the sole provider of food to this town. Why should he be the only one?"

"Then start your own farm," said Dana.

"And haven't you noticed that certain people seem to have all the wealth in this society?" continued Kenny. "And there are others who always seem to have nothing. Some of them are unable to work."

"But they're not starving," said Dana. "When a person falls on bad times in this place, the rest of us band together and help them get back on their feet if they want it."

"But you don't help Bert."

"Bert is a drunk," said Dana. "He spends all his time drinking and begging for a handout. People have offered him work, but he doesn't want it."

"That's not what he says."

"Kenny," Dana faced him, "I don't like where you are going with this. This is a good place where folk can be left alone to live as they see fit. No one here lives in fear of being arrested or their homes invaded by officers. A person here can work their way up if they choose. Or they can spend their days sitting on the sidewalk drinking and complaining about how unfair life is. Decisions are not made for them."

"You sound like the members of the resistance," Kenny's eyes darkened.

"And you have spent your entire life living in luxury, while speaking about fairness and equality of income."

"That's not fair and you know it."

"Was it fair that my parents were murdered?" Dana challenged. "Is it fair that back home, people's lives are determined for them?"

Dana heaved a huge sigh. "Kenny, you're my friend and I know we disagree on things, but please, do me a favor. Stay away from Bert and whatever he is talking you into doing. He's bad news."

"What do you mean?" asked Kenny.

"Kenny, I know you have lost everything and that you're scared. Bert is the sort of person that preys on such sentiments."

"I miss home," said Kenny.

"I do too."

"Really?"

"I don't miss the officers or all of the rules, but I miss the people. I miss Elsie and Sanders. And not a day goes by where I don't think about Jesse and Nana. Did they ever escape the fire?

"If you really want to go back, then I will take you back."

Kenny studied Dana's eyes. "You would, too."

"I need to get back," said Dana. "Um, Sampson has a spare room that you are welcome to use. Coming?"

"No, one of the guys here offered to let me stay with him."

Without warning, Kenny kissed Dana on the cheek. "You take care of yourself."

Dana stood frozen, staring after him. *Where did that come from?*

CHAPTER
SIXTEEN

Elsie and Sanders squirted through the chain-link fence blocking the alley. They had heard rumors about the resistance being in the area. Hoping to find it soon, they darted down the garbage-laden alley before any officers spotted them.

They entered a street. Quickly, they turned right and walked casually so as not to attract attention. Elsie noticed an officer doing his rounds. She took Sanders' hand into her own.

"What are you doing?" whispered Sanders.

"Just go with it. Pretend we're in love."

"What?"

"Just do it."

Finally realizing what Elsie meant, Sanders put his arm around her shoulders and placed her head on his own. He smiled and laughed while pretending to whisper words of love into her ear. In addition to his playacting, Elsie giggled like a schoolgirl.

The officer noted them. He tipped his hat as he strolled by what he believed to be two people hopelessly in love. Glancing behind, Sanders and Elsie rushed down the walk and turned another corner.

Sanders glanced at one of the gigantic television screens that dominated the city. Once again, the president's message that Dana was a dangerous criminal who needed to be stopped aired. Then, static took over until a new video appeared with the insignia of the resistance.

"Wait," he said to Elsie as he watched.

The song of the rebellion played while words darted across the screen.

Don't believe the lies.

They smear her because they fear her.

Dana's picture appeared on the screen again, but this time, she looked noble and proud.

All she did was ask a question.

All she did was try to save a friend.

And they have condemned her to death for it.

Carry the torch. Hold it high like Dana Ginary.

"What is all this?" asked Elsie as the screen went blank, and then Halloway appeared, apologizing for technical difficulties.

"She must still be alive," said Sanders, "and maybe the resistance knows where she is."

"Let's get out of here," said Elsie, pulling Sanders along. "We need to find them before the officers find us."

~ ~ ~

Dana walked down the main road, heading for Betsy's

diner to work. Since Malcolm wouldn't be back for weeks, she decided to continue working there for money.

She noticed a crowd gathering around someone speaking at a podium. It didn't take long for Dana to recognize Kenny's voice. Curious, she joined them and listened.

"We have rights as workers," said Kenny over the crowd, "and we deserve equal pay for equal work. People need a day off every now and then. Is that too much to ask?"

"No," said a few within the gathering.

"And why isn't there a fund to help take care of the old and infirmed? Sometimes, things happen and you find yourself unable to provide for your family. I propose that we set up a security fund that everyone pays into, and when you fall on hard times, money can be withdrawn from it to meet your needs until things improve.

"Why is it we have an attitude of 'too bad you lost your job, but don't ask me for anything'? That's pretty callous. We need to start thinking about the common good and about our community so that we all benefit."

Dana's heart sank as she listened. Apparently, Kenny refused her advice. She looked around at the various faces of the crowd. Most listened with rapt attention, with only a few openly agreeing.

Bert stood in the front, pretending to absorb everything Kenny said. He shouted cheers and agreements every so often, trying to get others to join him. Most of his efforts proved to be in vain.

"Betsy," exclaimed Dana as she ran into the woman who owned the diner. "What are you doing here?"

"Thought I'd come out and see what all the fuss was

about," said Betsy in her usual crass manner. "Most of what he says sounds reasonable."

Dana glanced at Kenny, who continued speaking. "It usually does." She remembered President Klens giving similar statements.

"Nincompoops," muttered Betsy. "Well, I got a business to run and you're late for work."

Dana followed Betsy to the diner, allowing Kenny's statements to fade. She hung up her coat and put on her apron, tying her hair into a bun.

"Now hurry up and get those counters cleaned," said Betsy.

"Yes, ma'am," said Dana. She had learned to ignore the woman's brusque manner.

The door rang as someone walked in.

"Hello, Mr. Callors," greeted Dana. "Eggs and ham this morning?"

"You know me too well," said Mr. Callors, taking off his hat. "Would you mind adding some of those biscuits with gravy?"

"I don't, but Betsy might."

"I don't know why I should make gravy for you," came Betsy's voice from the back. "Always making me do more work."

"So, how's Kenny doing at the stables?" asked Dana.

"I fired him," said Mr. Callors, "He left the job half done. Guess he thought the work was beneath him. Seems like he prefers to speak to crowds. Though what he's talking about is beyond me."

"Sorry to hear that," said Dana as she poured a cup of coffee.

"I know he's your friend, Dana, but it sounds like he's trying to cause trouble."

Dana frowned as she glanced outside at Kenny's animated motions. She started to wonder if perhaps he really was her friend. The thought that she needed to stay away from him entered her mind. "No need to apologize," she said.

"Order up," said Betsy.

Dana grabbed the plate and placed it in front of Mr. Callors. "Enjoy your meal."

"Thanks, dear." He picked up his fork and dug in.

Sampson walked in. "Coffee, please."

Dana gave him a cup with cream and sugar.

"Looks like trouble is brewing," he said.

Dana didn't respond.

"I don't know what that kid is working the people up for, but I do know that Bert is behind it."

"What makes you say that?" asked Dana.

"In all the time I've been here," answered Sampson, "Bert has been trying to get people to follow him. He is a lazy SOB who just wants what he thinks is owed to him. The thing is, most people ignore him because he spends all his time drinking. Now it seems he's sobered up and has snagged himself a new best friend. Yours."

"I've been thinking about that," said Dana.

"The thing is, he believes what he's saying," said Sampson.

"Yeah, he does," replied Dana, worry filling her.

She had hoped that if Kenny learned the value of hard work, he would appreciate it. She wanted him to understand what most in Dystopia understood, that people need to be allowed to live their own lives. Now she started to think it was a lost cause.

"I don't know what to tell you," said Dana. "Hopefully, this will all blow over."

"I hope so, but I have my doubts," said Sampson. "I might have to break it up."

"But people are allowed to meet in public," said Dana.

"They are," replied Sampson, "but not if it means they plan on starting a riot. If they take to what he says seriously, it could turn ugly. I suggest you stay close to the house and don't go wandering too much."

Dana frowned. She went back behind the counter and continued serving customers, all the while keeping a wary eye on Kenny and the ever increasing crowd.

The door jingled as Karl walked in. Goggles sat atop his white head as he strolled into the diner, oblivious to all the stares he garnered.

"Karl?" said Betsy. "You don't often leave your house."

"You didn't blow it up, did you?" asked Sampson.

"No. No," Karl waved their concerns away. "But I thought I could use some real homecooking for a change."

"Your stove not working?" asked Betsy.

"Not at the moment, no," replied Karl.

"What you do, set fire to it?" asked another in the diner.

"Actually," Karl turned to the man, "I needed a power source for this new invention of mine, so I hooked it up to my stove. When I turned it on, I fried both the invention and my stove. So here I am." Karl took two deep breaths while beating his fists against his chest. "Ah, smell that fresh air."

"That would be bacon," said Betsy.

"Well, be a dear and put some of it on a plate for me."

Karl leaned over the counter and kissed Betsy on the lips. In return, she smacked him hard across the face, leaving a red handprint on his cheek. Infuriated, Betsy stormed into the kitchen. Karl just smiled to himself with glee.

"Still got it," he muttered to himself.

"Got what?" Dana asked Sampson.

"That's what we've been trying to figure out," replied Sampson. "He lost his marbles a long time ago."

"Oh, Dana," Karl hurried over to her, "I need some coils for… uh… well, I need some coils about this big. Next time you go off with the traders, will you pick me up some? I'll pay you."

Dana thought a moment. She didn't mind helping Karl out. "I might know where I can get some without having to go far," she said. "I can bring them by sometime."

"Great!"

"Order up," Betsy plopped a bag with cartons of food on the counter.

Karl seized it eagerly. "Oh, that smells tantalizing."

"Enjoy, cuz I poisoned it," replied Betsy.

Karl wagged a finger at her. "You are a shrewd woman. But I will thoroughly enjoy this home cooked treat, even if it is my last meal on this earth. Oh, and Dana, just wait until you see my newest invention."

Karl skipped out the door. He took two more deep breaths before marching down the street.

"One of these days, that crazy old coot is going to blow himself up," said Betsy.

Sampson drank the last of his coffee. "Sometimes I wonder if he acts crazy on purpose. Well, I need to go. Thanks for the coffee."

Dana watched Sampson leave. She took one last look across the street at the crowd as more people joined, before turning back to her work.

~ ~ ~

Elsie and Sanders moved quickly despite the chilly rain as they trotted down the sidewalk and away from prying eyes. A door with red, peeling paint loomed before them. According to their information, this was the place where the resistance hid.

Cautiously, Elsie knocked on the door. She hoped that they had not been led into a trap. Footsteps sounded on the other side as someone approached, undoing the chains. Holding tightly onto one another, both Elsie and Sanders waited with baited breath.

The door opened a crack as a man peeked out. "What do you want?"

"Silent is the night where stands Lady Liberty," whispered Elsie.

The man looked around before shutting the door. More bolts and locks snapped out of place before it was wrenched open again. "In."

Quickly, Elsie and Sanders ran inside. They huddled together while looking around the dimly lit room. Several men and women looked back at them.

"All right, how'd you find us?" asked the man who had opened the door. He was Charles.

"We have sources," said Elsie.

"So do we," said Charles, "but that doesn't answer the question."

Sanders and Elise fidgeted while trying to think of how to answer.

"Well?"

"We asked around," said Sanders, "starting at the underground market. Some people there told us where we could find you. But you kept moving around, which made it a bit difficult."

"People there just told you?"

"His name was Phil," added Elsie.

"You fools," snapped Charles. "Did it ever occur to you that you might have been followed? That this might have been a trap?"

Both Elsie and Sanders shook their heads. They had never considered the possibility.

"Of course not. Dumb kids."

"Now, Charles," said Simon, "hold your temper in check. They don't look like they work for Colonel Fernau."

"No, of course not," muttered Charles. "Just that stupid kid, Dana, did."

"Dana isn't stupid," Elsie blurted out.

"Well she certainly got us all in a tight fix," said Charles. "And George is dead because of her."

"Dana was coerced," said Simon, "and George knew the risks when he decided to go with her. Now, Amy, will you get these two something to eat?"

Amy nodded and went to the kitchen. Moments later, she returned with two steaming bowls of soup.

"Now, tell us how you got out of the plant," said Simon.

"We ran away during the riot," Elsie replied around a mouthful of food. "Been running ever since."

"How is it you managed to steer clear of the officers? Ever since Dana's speech, their numbers have increased."

"That part gets tricky," said Sanders. "We bribed a number of them, but mostly, we stay out of sight. During the nights, we stay in abandoned buildings. Nighttime is the only time we move, if we can help it."

"How is it they haven't tracked you?" asked Charles.

In response, both Elsie and Sanders held out their arms, re-vealing the healing cuts from where they had dug out their chips.

"Good thinking," conceded Charles.

"Look," said Elsie, "we can't go back to Waste Manage-ment. You know what will happen to us if we do. We want to join you."

"Join us?"

"Yes," replied Sanders.

"We believe in what you are trying to achieve," added Elsie. "We can help."

"How?" demanded Charles.

"Those videos you air by hacking into the media network. How many times have you had to relocate after airing them?"

The stony expressions on their faces told Elsie she had struck a nerve.

"Sanders is the best person with a computer that I know. He managed to hack their system the day Dana escaped. It was him who played the video of her interrogations, and he set it up so it was traced back to Officer Burroughs."

"I heard they had executed him," said Amy.

"Sanders here can hack the network and make it look like it came from anywhere. It doesn't mean that we won't have to stay on the move, but maybe we won't have to move as often."

"That is worth considering," mused Simon.

"We've got no place to go and you know it," said Sanders.

"And if we found you once, we can find you again," Elsie added.

The people within the room gathered together, whispering to one another. After several minutes, Simon silenced them.

"Okay, you can stay," he said, "but you must abide by our rules. You cannot leave without permission. You must keep quiet and not attract attention. The officers are everywhere these days, and they would want nothing more than to hang all of us."

"Yeah, and President Klens is expected to issue new regulations concerning people's activities," said Amy.

"I heard she was real angry when Dana took off," laughed Charles.

"I think that is putting it mildly," said Amy. "You've seen those propaganda pieces. They're doing everything to smear her."

"That's enough," Simon interrupted them. "We have a lot of planning to do before our next airing. You two get some sleep."

Elsie and Sanders finished their meal before following a small, almost timid woman to their new accommodations while affectionately holding one another's hands.

~ ~ ~

Dana stepped out into the ever increasing chilly air as she locked up the diner. Betsy had taken to letting her close up for the evening. Dana knew enough about cooking by now to handle the few small orders that came in.

She stuck the key in the lock and smiled when it clicked. As Dana headed down the street for the road that led to Sampson's, she wished she had the truck. He had needed it to check on his fields. Because it was warm that morning, Dana said walking wouldn't be a problem. *If only I had remembered how quickly the weather can change.*

"Hey," said Kenny walking up to her.

"Hi," said Dana.

"Can I walk you home?"

Dana paused and looked at her friend in the moonlight. For the first time, she saw him as a man. She didn't know why she hadn't noticed it before, but he no longer appeared as the scrawny kid from school. He had filled out some.

"What is it?" asked Kenny.

"Nothing," said Dana, shaking such thoughts from her head. They frightened her.

"So can I walk you home?"

"Why do you want to walk me home?"

"Because it's nighttime and I know there are dangerous people about. I heard about the men that had kidnapped you."

"All right then. Come on."

Together, they walked down the road, turning onto the dirt highway that went to Sampson's. Though about five miles, Dana didn't mind walking, so long as it wasn't too cold.

"I saw you today giving your speech to the crowd," said Dana breaking the silence.

"What did you think of it?"

Dana didn't answer immediately.

"Didn't you like it?"

"Yes and no," said Dana.

"What was wrong with it?" asked Kenny.

"Parts of it sounded good and made sense."

"But you still have your doubts."

"How many times have we heard in school that the common good should never be ignored? How many times have we heard about equality? But they didn't exist there. You know that."

"I just want to live in a place where everyone is able to live as they were meant to, free and without hardship. That was the point of Dystopia."

"Well, something went terribly wrong," said Dana.

"But we can fix that here," Kenny replied.

"But people are free here," said Dana. "For the first time, I don't feel afraid."

"But there is hardship. I hear that some years, people here don't have much to eat and are completely reliant on what your friend Sampson grows."

"He doesn't charge much and most don't have to pay until things improve."

"But it's the unfairness of life I want to eliminate."

"You'll never be able to do that," said Dana. "Look, Kenny, I admire what you're trying to do, but I think you're going about it the wrong way. You believe in the principles you were raised in, but you never experienced the other side of that coin.

"We have equality here. Everyone is equal before the law and expected to follow the same set of rules. Anyone can find a job here of their own choosing if they have a mind to. And right now, you and I are walking down this road alone and there isn't an officer in sight. People here have a pretty good life. I'm not saying it isn't without its problems, but I don't think what you're doing is going to help much."

"That's not what Bert says."

Dana's expression clouded. "You know how I feel about Bert."

"Why don't you like him?"

"I just have this bad feeling about him. He's a good for nothing..."

"You're judging."

"Everyone judges."

"So I guess you won't be coming to hear me speak tomorrow night," said Kenny.

"What?" asked Dana.

"You said that if I didn't like the current mayor, that I should run for the position myself. Well, Sampson is up for reelection."

"But the vote is weeks away."

"Yeah, but I checked the rules, and anyone can enter their name into the race up until the day before the voting."

"You don't have any experience," said Dana.

"I have plenty," replied Kenny, "I was the First Councilman's son."

Dana didn't think that meant much, but she kept her mouth shut. "Just be careful what you say, Kenny."

"What do you mean?"

"Words mean things and can be used to convince people to do terrible acts."

"Don't worry about me."

It wasn't Kenny she was worried about. "We're here," said Dana, surprised that the walk had gone so quickly.

"Please come tomorrow," pleaded Kenny.

"Maybe I'll stop by near the end," Dana relented.

"Good. Then we can grab some dinner." He pecked her on the cheek and walked away waving as he left.

Dana stood erect unsure of what to think. Kenny had never openly showed feelings for her, but then back home, he couldn't have, even if he wanted to. For the second time that night, she thought of him as a man. Though he aggravated her on many levels, Dana knew his affection towards her was genuine.

She turned and headed to the house, hoping she was not headed for trouble.

CHAPTER

SEVENTEEN

President Klens sat behind her desk, trying to read the reports that had been brought to her. Seth Michaels and the First Councilman of the western region, Donald Humphries, stood before her. She had summoned a meeting with both of them in her Los Angeles residence. Despite her efforts, riots continued to spring up.

Music flowed in from the open window as people marched in the streets.

> *Fires burning.*
> *Children crying.*
> *The Lady stands alone.*

"What is that inferno song?" demanded President Klens.

"It is one of the songs from the rebellion. It is also the song that the protesters of 11 years ago sang," replied Seth Michaels.

"Well shut that window," snapped President Klens. "I want a stop put to it."

"Protest?" said Donald.

"Yes," replied Seth Michaels. "Dana Ginary's grandfather was part of that gathering. She was there too."

"Oh, that poor girl. To witness such horror at such a young…" Donald Humphries stopped speaking when he noticed the irate expression on President Klens' face.

"Sorry, Madam President," he apologized.

"How did you ever get the position of First Councilman?" President Klens asked him.

"It was given to me," he replied, "after my father died and vacated the seat."

"You are aware that you can be replaced at any time?"

Donald Humphries tugged at his collar as sweat formed on his neck. "Yes, ma'am."

"And as for the riots in the eastern region," continued President Klens, "how are you dealing with them?"

"Madam President, the moment we put one down, another springs up," said Seth Michaels.

"I don't want excuses!" President Klens shrill voice rattled the walls. "And as for that little wretch, I want her dead!"

President Klens walked over to a window and looked out. A line of people openly marched in front of her house, carrying a poster with Dana's picture while singing their song. "Why do they follow her?"

"Because she gives them hope," said Seth Michaels.

"Hope?"

"She openly defied you, and defied our government."

"She took your little plan," said President Klens, "and slapped you in the face with it."

"The more we broadcast those fals—I mean, reports about her, the more the people disbelieve them," said Donald Humphries.

"I want her destroyed. I want her found!"

"You won't need to find her," Colonel Fernau entered the room, "She will come to us."

"Colonel Fernau," said President Klens with surprise, "I didn't see you standing there."

"Silence has its uses," replied Colonel Fernau in a silky tone.

"What do you have in mind?" asked President Klens.

"There are many small settlements in the wastelands. They are tiny and primitive, but they are able to receive many of our broadcasts. I suggest we air a message. One that only she will understand, but will force her to come back to Dystopia."

"Are you certain that she will take the bait?" asked the president.

"Oh, I'm sure she will," said Colonel Fernau with a malicious smile.

"And as for that crowd," said President Klens, pointing at those marching in the street.

"Already taken care of," said Colonel Fernau.

President Klens looked back out the window as armed officers marched into the streets. They raised their weapons and opened fire. Terrified screams rose up from below as people darted in every direction. Gunfire continued to pummel them until only silence remained.

President Klens smiled to herself as she turned back to the men within her office. "You gentlemen are dismissed."

Seth Michaels and Donald Humphries nodded and left.

"Oh, Colonel," said President Klens, "I think it's time we have a new First Councilman for the western region."

Colonel Fernau saluted. He marched out of the office and into the hallway. "Mr. Humphries," he said as he put an arm around the man, "might I have a word with you?"

"Yes, Colonel," said Donald Humphries. "What can I do for you?"

"I was wondering how you would handle a stressful situation." Colonel Fernau led the man to a balcony.

"I'm not sure what you mean."

"Well, for instance, how would you deal with this?"

Colonel Fernau pushed Donald Humphries over the rail. He reveled in the man's screams until they came to an abrupt end with a sickening thud. He peered over the railing at the bloodied corpse below.

"Not very well at all."

The voice of a lone woman caught his attention. He looked up at her as she cradled a man in her arms and sang. He didn't know where the song had come from, but he listened to it anyway.

People are we
who just wish to live free.
Lives that should be our own,
yet the Nanny won't leave us alone.

Terrorists we are branded.
Rights we aren't granted.
Our mouths have been sealed
so that truth will ne'er be revealed.

Character is our identity

not a group's anonymity.
Our choice our responsibility.
But robbed we are of liberty.

Curse me; hate me if you will.
My voice shall never be stilled.
Spout your lies. Tarnish my name.
Your hands bear evil's stain.

The woman stared defiantly at Colonel Fernau when she sang the last line. They locked eyes for a moment. Determined will filled her eyes as she looked at him.

Callously, Colonel Fernau pulled out his gun and shot her. *One less piece of garbage.* He holstered his weapon and went back inside.

CHAPTER EIGHTEEN

Dana entered the building where the meeting took place. The massive crowd took her breath away. Kenny's message had spread rapidly, attracting all sorts of new faces. She had never thought that it would catch on so quickly. Dana squeezed her way through the throng of people toward the front. She paused when she reached the stage.

As she listened to Kenny's speech, Dana had to admit that he was a powerful speaker. Amidst the cheers and applause, all Dana got from Kenny's message was that people agreed with him. Despite their lack of substance, his words hypnotized and unnerved her. She spotted Bert, who stood off to the side with a satisfied smile.

"When we all get a fair shot, we all succeed," Kenny droned on. "When every person has access to a good paying job, we all succeed. When we all have affordable medical care, we all benefit. No one is above or beneath you. We are all equal and deserve to have our needs met. It is time for the ones with all the wealth to quit being selfish and to share with the rest of us.

"There is no such thing as Sammy's store or Johnny's property because it is the people's property. After all, we are part of a community; therefore, what we have belongs to all of us. When one of us succeeds, the entire group succeeds. Why should we sacrifice the community just for the sake of an individual's selfish desires?

"After all, that store over there. It may be Mr. Harris', but he didn't build it on his own. You—all of you shop there, and therefore, helped build it. If you didn't spend your hard earned money there, he would not have a business. If those of you who helped build this road hadn't, he would not have that store. Because it services our needs, we all helped build it.

"Greed is what put you on the streets. By working together for the common good, we will all have a place to call home.

"I am talking about our rights. Your rights! You have a right to a home. A right to health care. A right to a job that provides for your needs. A right to live comfortably. A right to security. A right to adequate food."

Kenny spotted Dana in the front. She immediately wished he hadn't.

"And my friend, Dana, there agrees with me. She knows what it is like to be exploited by selfish individuals who care only for their ends."

Dana tried backing away, but the packed crowd refused to let her escape. Before she knew it, Kenny had hopped off the stage, snatched her arm, and hauled her in front of the microphone.

"Kenny, no," Dana pleaded trying to pull away.

"Come on," said Kenny. "Just tell the truth."

"You won't like what I have to say," she hissed.

Kenny ignored her pleas, too wrapped up in the moment. Before Dana could pull away, she had been thrust in front of the microphone, finding herself staring into the faces of hopeful and expectant people for the second time in her life. She glanced at Kenny, who motioned for her to speak.

"Kenny was correct when he said that I had been used by selfish individuals, but not in the way you think. I come from a place where everything you do is controlled by a government that cares only about its own ends and not those it is sworn to protect. I was raised listening to these same sentiments."

Dana glanced back at Kenny, his face seething. *You wanted me to speak.*

"But I do not agree with them. If you follow what he and Bert are promoting, it will lead you to your destruction."

Bert snatched the microphone from her. "But you admit that it isn't right for one man to exploit another."

"Bert, before you found someone to use as your puppet, no one cared about you. Now, suddenly, you are an important figure in this town. So who's really being selfish?"

Bert raised his hand to Dana. She caught it in midswing.

"Don't ever do that again," she said, her words echoing around them. Dana walked away from the scene, disgusted with each of them.

"I told you not to make me speak," she hissed at Kenny as she passed him.

"Dana!"

She kept walking.

"Dana!"

Kenny skidded to a halt in front of her, forcing her to stop. She glared at him.

"What was that all about?" demanded Kenny.

"I told you not to put me in front of the microphone."

"But you totally disagreed with me in there."

"You knew I never agreed with your speeches," said Dana. "Why did you drag me up there in the first place?"

"Because I saw you standing there and I thought that maybe you finally understood things."

"Kenny," Dana sighed, "I always liked you as a friend. Despite our differences, we somehow managed to get along. But now I can see that we are completely different. You've chosen your path and I've chosen mine."

"What do you mean?"

Shouts and jeers rose up from within the gathering hall as Bert worked the people into a frenzy. Whatever Dana had said was forgotten.

"You better get back in there," said Dana. "Your captivated audience waits."

"Dana, I want you with me. We can change this place together."

"I never wanted to change it," said Dana. "I hope you like the harvest from the seeds you have sown."

"Dana…"

"Good-bye, Kenny."

Dana ran away before Kenny could see her tears. She mourned the loss of a friend, of a person she wondered if she ever really knew.

~ ~ ~

Three adolescent boys strolled down the street, talking amongst themselves.

"That Kenny guy is right," said one.

"About what?" asked another.

"Well, you know," replied the first. "About how we all deserve a decent living. How we all should be given a fair wage and should be allowed to have the things we need to live."

"Yeah, but don't we already have that?" asked the third, timidly.

"Whose side are you on?" demanded the first. "After all, my dad ain't had anything since he lost his job. Why should we have to suffer because no one wants to hire him?"

"Yeah," said the second. "Look at that diner over there." He pointed at Betsy's diner. "She kicked me out because I refused to pay for my meal. I have to eat, so why should I have to pay for my food?"

"Exactly," said the first.

"Yeah," added the third teenager in a quiet voice. He didn't quite agree with his friends, but did not want to be ostracized either.

"She's just one of those greedy capitalists who makes her living on the backs of the poor," said the first teenager.

"Yeah," agreed the second. "We should teach her a lesson and take what we're owed."

"It's time to get ours," said the first.

One of the teenagers picked up a stone. Taking careful aim, he threw it at the window to Betsy's diner. The glass shattered as shards of it tingled on the boarded walkway.

Betsy burst from the diner, shaking her fist. "What in blazes do you three think you're doing? You'll have to pay for that!"

"We ain't paying for nothing!" yelled the first teenager. "You've been making your living off us for too long."

"Yeah, it's time you give us what we're owed, you greedy whore," said the second, joining his friend.

They scooped up globs of mud and flung it at Betsy. She brought her hands up in an effort to block the attack before escaping inside.

"Come on," the first two turned to their friend. "You're either with us or against us."

Not wanting to be on the receiving end of their anger, the third teenager grabbed some mud and chucked it at Betsy's diner. "Power to the downtrodden!"

After several minutes, the three boys stopped their rampage and ran off. As their shouts and yells faded, Betsy remained in her diner, hunkering in the kitchen, afraid to come out.

CHAPTER

NINETEEN

"I got you the coils you wanted," Dana said to Karl, the mad scientist of the town.

Karl skipped over to her with excitement as he grabbed them. "Thank you. I've been waiting a long time for these."

Karl's enthusiasm never ceased to amaze Dana. She always marveled at how, for an old man, he managed to hop around like a six-year-old, his white hair and whiskers flailing all over the place.

"So what's the news around town?" Karl asked.

"Well, Bert and Kenny seem satisfied to get people all riled up over nothing," replied Dana.

"Some of them have real grievances," said Karl as he fiddled with some glass tube and a weird coil inside it.

"Maybe," said Dana, "but I never thought life was that bad here."

"And some still don't."

Karl trampled around on the paper-covered floor as he searched for something. "Ah, found it," he said, pulling out a pair of pliers.

"What exactly are you building?" asked Dana.

"Nothing."

"It doesn't look like nothing." She noted the bubbly red liquid within the glass tube.

"Well," said Karl, "I'm trying to figure out how to use the energy of the planet to create a better energy source for our town."

"Sorry?"

"Honestly, did you pay any attention in school?" Karl looked at Dana as though she were the dumbest person on the planet.

"Yeah, but we didn't discuss anything…"

"The earth generates its own energy and magnetic field," said Karl. "I believe that it is possible to tap that and use it to generate electricity. Then we wouldn't be so dependent on the panels or generators."

"But you invented those generators."

"Yes, but I believe in having more than one way of doing things."

Karl grabbed Dana and led her to another part of the laboratory room.

"See those tubes? They go deep within the earth. I dug the holes years ago. These coils you brought me are the last piece I need to connect them to that."

Karl pointed to the glass tube in his workroom.

"This thing isn't going to blow up, is it?" asked Dana.

"It might," Karl shrugged. "Here. You might want these." He handed her a pair of goggles. Unsure of the situation,

Dana took them and put them on, thinking she ought to put some distance between her and Karl's strange new invention.

"Karl, how long have you been working on this?" asked Dana.

"Years," replied Karl. "I know it can be done. I just haven't figured out how yet. Just when I think I have discovered the last piece of the puzzle, something goes wrong."

"And you keep working at it."

"Why wouldn't I?" Karl looked at Dana as though she had said something completely idiotic.

"Most would have given up."

"Because most people don't understand the value of working for something," said Karl. "This is my life's work, and I'm going to keep at it until I achieve my goal or die. Whichever comes first."

Dana peeked out the grimy window at the people gathered outside, listening to another of Kenny's speeches.

"You see them out there?" asked Karl. "They have either given up or they feel that they shouldn't have to work anymore."

Dana listened to the shouts from the crowd. "They sound angry."

"Probably because they are," said Karl. "It doesn't take much to work people into a frenzy. A place can be peaceful where the people there are happy. Then one day, a man can walk in and get everyone worked up where they are full of anger and hatred toward one another. It isn't hard. Anger and hatred are the easiest emotions to fall prey to."

"So why are they letting him do it?" asked Dana.

"Because they don't realize that he is. That boy has been giving a lot of pretty speeches that sound good. And those people have been getting worked up over it and they don't even know why. And then those who don't like what he's saying get mad at the ones who are listening to him. I've seen it many times."

"What do you mean?"

"Honey, I've been on this earth for 75 years. In all that time, I have been to places that were peaceful and the people content. Then someone like your friend showed up, and before we knew it, we were at each other's throats. I left before things got too ugly."

"What happened to that place?" asked Dana.

"It doesn't exist anymore."

Dana remained silent as she watched Karl fiddle with his machine.

"Ready to see if it works?" asked Karl.

"Uh, I think I'm going to go."

"Nonsense," said Karl, pulling her over. "It's perfectly safe."

He flipped the switch. Immediately, the machine whistled and sputtered as it rattled the table it sat on. The red liquid inside bubbled and boiled with a vengeance. Then, nothing.

"You piece of…"

Dana listened as Karl released a stream of curses she had never heard before. She waited patiently for him to finish.

"Not even one spark!"

Karl kicked his machine. It hummed to life, whistling and sputtering some more as the mechanism turned. On and on it went, building in intensity. A spark of electricity shot from the machine and down a wire to the lone light bulb that had been hooked up to it.

Dana watched as the bulb lit up. Smiles crossed both hers and Karl's faces. They clapped each other on the back, thrilled that the invention worked.

The light bulb burst. Suddenly, the machine made loud, ominous noises as it began rattling strongly enough to shake the entire house.

"Dana," said Karl. "I think we should leave. Like now."

"What?"

Karl pushed and shoved Dana toward the front door as the smoke filled the laboratory and more glass tubes shattered. Karl stopped. He remembered his charts and diagrams. Instantly, he ran to his study to retrieve them.

"Karl!" Dana ran after him.

"I need these," said Karl as he pulled all sorts of papers off the shelves.

"But you said…"

"I know what I said," shouted Karl over the ever increasing noise.

Finally, Dana dragged Karl away from his study and threw him out the door. Together, they ran to the edge of his property as the ground shook beneath their feet. They turned to observe everything.

The house continued to vibrate, the windows rattling. When it seemed as though it was about to explode, a small hissing sound escaped and everything stilled.

"That's it?" said Karl, throwing up his hands and scattering papers all around him and Dana. "After all that, that's it? Geez, not even a…"

CRACK-KABOOM!

The explosion knocked them off their feet as smoke burst through the shattered windows. A good-sized hole appeared in the roof. Karl tossed up his arms, dancing and singing with joy at the mess.

"Woo-hoo! That was a big one! I must really be onto something. That was fantastic!"

"Fantastic?" said Dana. "You almost completely destroyed your house."

"I know! Isn't it wonderful?"

Karl darted off, singing and dancing to himself as he reentered his house. Perplexed and a bit worried about the man's sanity, Dana watched him leave. She turned and headed in the opposite direction, having had enough of explosive science experiments.

The sounds of the gathered crowd drew Dana's attention. She wandered over to them, curious about what was being said now.

"I propose a system where there are no distinctions among us, as we are all one," came Kenny's voice. "We must take back what is ours."

"Take back what?" asked Sampson, his voice drowning Kenny's and the crowd.

"Mayor," said one. "What are you doing here?"

"There's been a lot of noise lately."

"We have every right to gather," said Bert.

"True," replied Sampson, "but it sounds like you all are fixing for a fight. So I ask you again, what has been taken from you that you feel you must fight to get it back?"

No one answered.

"What are you doing here, mayor?" asked another.

"When people start acting like a mob, it gets my attention. When people start breaking the law, it deserves my attention," said Sampson.

"No one here has broken the law."

"Really?" said Sampson. "Someone, yesterday, threw a rock through Betsy's window with the words 'greedy exploiter' written on it. Now she has to pay to have that fixed."

"She's got money," said Bert. "Let her pay for it."

A few agreements came from the crowd.

"Except she shouldn't have to," said Sampson. "Whoever threw that rock had no right to damage her property."

"It should be the community's property," said Kenny. "We all own it."

"Did you purchase the building?" asked Sampson. "Did any of you clean it up and fix it up to make it habitable? Did any of you purchase the food that is prepared and then served? Do any of you who eat there wash the dishes afterward? No. Betsy does all of that."

"But we do pay her to eat there," said a young man who looked to be no more than 15 years old.

"And that gives you claim to it?" asked Sampson.

The kid didn't answer.

"Now I don't know what has happened to make you all think that you need to act like a bunch of criminals to get what you want," said Sampson. "We have a city council to which any of you may take your grievances and have them addressed. There are more peaceful means to right any wrongs you think you may have suffered. But this—all of this—has got to stop before someone gets hurt."

"No one is going to get hurt," said Kenny. "We are not violent people."

"Someone always gets hurt when men choose to abandon reason and civility for emotion and madness."

"Mayor," asked a woman as Sampson turned to leave, "when will Betsy reopen her diner?"

"She isn't," said Sampson. "She's closing it indefinitely."

"How will anyone be able to eat there?"

"The person who threw the rock should have thought about that before giving into his whims."

Dana hurried away from the scene. She watched as Bert put an arm around Kenny's shoulders and whispered into his ear. Anger filled Dana as she watched them. Quickly, she turned and ran down the street towards Mr. Callors' stables to see her horse. He had told her she could keep him there indefinitely. Dana appreciated having a place she knew her horse would be cared for.

Pausing by the general store, Dana purchased a couple of apples. "Thank you," she said to the clerk as she darted off with her treat for Poboy.

She knew she shouldn't spoil her horse too much, but Dana had never had a pet before. She turned and trotted along as the stable appeared larger the closer she got. Passing by a group of people regurgitating one of Kenny's many speeches, she frowned.

Ignoring them, she continued on until she entered the stable, spotting Poboy immediately. The horse recognized her, snorting and pawing the ground as she approached.

"Hey, boy," she said softly. "How's my Poboy?"

The horse snorted.

Smiling, Dana reached up and petted his muzzle, amazed at how soft the fur was. "I brought you something."

Poboy neighed excitedly, knowing what the bag contained.

Dana pulled out the two apples and held them in her hand. She watched as her horse ate the fruit, careful not to harm her. Once done, she wiped the saliva on her pants. Poboy looked at her expectantly, as though she should have more.

"That's it," said Dana. "You ate it all."

The horse snorted in disappointment.

"Maybe you should get a job and buy your own apples."

Poboy shook his head, tossing his mane around.

"All right, you silly thing." Dana stroked his muzzle again. "You know, there are some strange things going on. There seems to be a lot of anger out there. I don't even know where it's coming from. But Kenny—you remember him—he's stirring it up. Of course, he's not alone. That Bert seems to be behind it all."

Dana paused and looked into Poboy's brown eyes. He nuzzled into her. Chuckling, she stroked him some more.

"I'll never understand it," continued Dana. "I'll never understand why some believe that they deserve what another has. Or why they let themselves be used."

"Well, that is a puzzle that has plagued many a man," said Mr. Callors as he walked in.

Startled, Dana jumped at the sound of his voice.

"Didn't mean to frighten you," said Mr. Callors. "I noticed the door was open, so I came in to make sure everything was okay."

"I can leave," started Dana.

"Stay. He's your horse. It's good you come here regularly. He'd get lonesome if you didn't."

"I was just talking to him."

"Go right ahead and talk to him," said Mr. Callors. "You see those eyes? There's intelligence there. Animals understand everything we say. Sometimes they seem to know what we're thinking before we know it ourselves.

"Now this stall. This was where I kept Valor. He was a good horse. Strong too."

"What happened to him?" asked Dana.

"He got old," replied Mr. Callors. "Then he got sick and I had to put him down. I couldn't bear to see him suffering.

Your Poboy there reminds me a lot of him. Independently minded and stubborn. A lot like you, I'd say."

Dana smiled.

"Well, you stay as long as you like. Just make sure you lock up when you're done. There's been a lot of strange things going on lately. Don't trust anyone anymore."

"Thank you, Mr. Callors."

Dana watched him leave as she continued to scratch Poboy's mane. The horse neighed with delight. "You like that, don't you?"

Poboy snorted again and Dana kissed him on his muzzle.

"I've got to go now," said Dana, "but I'll be back."

She filled the horse's feeding trough and water. A harsh whinny made her turn around as she tried to leave. "Don't worry, I'll remember the apples."

Poboy nodded to indicate that she better remember them. "Night, boy."

Dana shut the door, firmly pleased that the lock clicked into place. Noticing the darkened sky, she realized that it was later than she thought. She hurried down the road toward the highway to Sampson's hoping she made it back before Minny started worrying.

A commotion caught her attention. Quickly, Dana headed for it knowing that something wasn't right. She approached the walk and paused as the same group of boys she had seen earlier wrecked the hot dog stand. They tossed it to the ground breaking it. Hot dogs and buns scattered everywhere. One of the boys picked up a ketchup bottle. He squirted the liquid all over the stand and the man who owned it.

"Hey! Stop that!" Dana ran for the poor man and chased the boys away. The boys laughed and joked among themselves as they fled, pleased with what they had done.

"Are you okay?" asked Dana.

"No," said the man, "Why'd they do that?"

"Just a bunch of punks."

"Stuff like this never happened before. They said I was selfish for wanting to own my own business. Called me all sorts of things and for what?"

"I'll help you clean it up," said Dana, unsure of what to say.

"Don't bother," said the man. "I can't sell this stuff now. It's ruined, and I don't have the funds to replace it. What am I going to tell my wife?"

Dana didn't answer. She had none.

"We have a baby on the way. Our first. I started this stand as a way to earn enough to provide for us. Never got much, but we had food and I owned my own life. Now look at it."

"You can rebuild it," encouraged Dana.

Her words sounded hollow even to her. The man looked defeated, a look she had seen many times back home.

"I don't know," said the man. "I need to go home and think." He left Dana alone on the sidewalk.

Footsteps sounded behind her. Whirling around, Dana came face to face with Kenny. "I hope you're happy."

"I'm not responsible for this," said Kenny. "Those boys did it."

"They were repeating your words, Kenny," snapped Dana. "You demonized people like him, and now others have gotten it in their heads to get rid of him. You are at least somewhat responsible."

"You can't blame me for the actions of another," Kenny shot back.

"Maybe not," said Dana, "but your words influenced them. What are you hoping to achieve?"

"Equality," said Kenny. "Justice."

Dana glanced at the mess on the ground. "Where is the justice in this? I'm sorry I ever saved you."

"You did it because we were friends."

"Yeah," said Dana, "we were once. But the Kenny I knew is gone. You've become your father."

Dana walked away, leaving Kenny alone in the night. She no longer cared what he did.

~ ~ ~

Colonel Fernau stood outside the doors to the underground market.

"We are ready, sir," said an officer.

"Proceed." The colonel's coldness sent shivers down the officer's spine.

Within moments, officers with a battering ram rushed the door. They waited a second before slamming it into the metal doors. Bang! The harsh sound reverberated off the walls around them. They rammed it into the doors again, causing the hinges to pop. A third time and the metal doors burst open, revealing an enclave of frightened people rushing about, desperate to get away.

Officers ran into the underground market, their weapons raised. Shouts and screams rose up as people hurried about. A slew of gunfire filled Colonel Fernau's ears with sweet music, causing him to smile slightly.

"We are ready to round them up and take them to the detention center," said an officer.

"Round them up?" Colonel Fernau turned to the officer. "Why would we round them up? They are worthless."

"Sir?"

"Kill them all."

"But, sir, they are people," challenged the officer.

"People? They are not people. They are traitors and should be treated as such," snarled Colonel Fernau, growing more irritated at the delay in obedience. "Traitors have no rights. Execute them, or I'll have you taken out and shot for disobeying direct orders."

"Yes, sir," saluted the officer. He darted off.

Immediately, rapid gunfire sounded. Colonel Fernau grinned as people scrambled about to get away. Bodies littered the ground in pools of blood. The shrill scream of a woman caught his attention. She ran out of the building with a dead child in her arms. Once outside, the woman paused. Weeping, she held her child out to Colonel Fernau, her eyes asking why. In response, Colonel Fernau pulled out his pistol and shot her. "Stupid wretches," he muttered.

More officers marched into the warehouse, dressed in full body armor. They raised their weapons, and upon the colonel's orders, opened fire. A rain of bullets flew through the area. Purposefully, Colonel Fernau strolled into the underground market, admiring his handiwork. He callously stepped on the lifeless forms beneath his heavy boots, not caring that they were alive moments before.

A flicker of movement on the far end caught his attention. "Quick, don't let them escape!"

Quickly, officers raced to where some scrambled towards a secret exit. Shots echoing around him meant that they had been killed.

Slowly, the screams died. Surveying the area, a sense of

accomplishment filled Colonel Fernau. "What a waste," he said as he kicked a corpse.

"Everyone has been subdued," said an officer.

"Burn it," ordered Colonel Fernau.

The officer saluted. Within minutes, a fire team marched inside with lit flamethrowers. Low rolls of thunder filled the room as they lit the place on fire. Within moments, the debris, bodies, and vendors sparked to life as flames engulfed them. Colonel Fernau remained poised among the inferno, reveling in the moment of his triumph. Tendrils of flames licked at his boots. Realizing it was time to leave, he stalked out of the underground market and into the cold night air.

A fitting end to garbage, he thought to himself.

"Colonel," said an officer as he ran up to the man with an electronic pad. "The communications center called. They think they found her."

Colonel Fernau snatched the pad from him. He studied the image. It looked like Dana, but the small screen made discerning the features difficult. He shoved the pad back into the officer's hands. "I will go there now. Tell them to expect my arrival shortly."

"Yes, sir."

A black car pulled up. Colonel Fernau ripped the door opened and settled inside. With a slight lurch, the car pulled away. Colonel Fernau rubbed his gloved hands together, hoping that he had finally found his quarry. *She will be mine.*

CHAPTER TWENTY

Dana sat on the porch swing with the book in her hands. The light in the window behind her shed enough on the pages for her to read. She liked reading outside in the dark. No one ever disturbed her.

The gritty and crinkled pages tickled her fingers as she turned them. As she read, Dana soon realized why this book was considered contraband back home. It proposed ideas contrary to what President Klens would ever allow. Though she thought Patrick Henry a bit too inflammatory for her taste, Dana thought he had relevant ideas. Among them was the idea that individuals should not be ruled by any governing body.

Voices caught her attention. Looking up, she noticed torches in the distance drawing closer. Dana shut the book and put it aside. As the marching feet drew nearer, she stood up and leaned on the rail.

Dana stared out at the distance and the town that lay before her. The inflamed shouts of a group of people as they increasingly grew angry unnerved her. She had never seen a populace so angry over something they couldn't even explain themselves. Spirals of smoke appeared. Light appeared as explosions took place. Dana watched the flashes of light appear.

Shapes moved down the road toward the house. Peering into the darkness, Dana realized that the people coming for them were not there on a friendly visit. She ran into the house.

"Sampson, we have company."

Sampson and Minny stepped outside. He took one look at the crowd and ran back into the house, rummaging around until he came back with his gun. Quickly, Sampson checked it, making certain it was loaded.

"Back in the house, both of you," said Sampson to Dana and Minny.

Reluctantly, the two women went back inside, turning off the lights. Dana stayed close to a window, watching everything.

As the sounds of marching feet drew nearer, an ominous feeling filled Dana. The expressions on the mob's faces told her that nothing good would come from all of this. She watched as Kenny and Bert led them to Sampson's front porch.

"What's the meaning of all this?" demanded Sampson when they got within earshot.

"You know," said Bert.

"No, I don't."

"We've come to right the injustices of this world," said one within the crowd.

"What injustices are you referring to?" demanded Sampson, cocking his weapon.

"These people don't have much," said Kenny. "We're here to give them their equal share."

"Equal share of what?" Sampson's voice had a sharp edge.

"You know full well what," said Bert. "It's not fair you having all this property and everything on it. It's not right that you control all of it. Many of us here can barely feed ourselves and yet you live in plenty."

"Have I not sold my crops at honest prices? Many times, one of you couldn't afford to pay me, yet I gave it to you anyway."

"Well, yeah, but it's not right you having so much."

"And who are you to decide that?" demanded Sampson. "This is my land. I have spent my life working it, and I'll be damned if I give it up to your lot."

"We just want what we are owed," shouted one.

Sampson raised his gun. "Oh, I'll give you that."

"Look, Sampson," said Kenny, "we don't want any violence. We just want an equal share for everyone. We are all part of this community and we all depend upon your farm for food. Therefore, we all deserve a share of it. Together, we'll make it richer."

"Take your nonsense elsewhere. I'm not giving up what is rightfully mine."

Before Dana knew what had happened, shots rang out as the mob stormed the house. Men piled on top of Sampson. Despite his strength and size, they quickly subdued him.

She and Minny raced for the back door. Before they reached it, people burst inside from all entry points. Minny grabbed Dana and tried to pull her to the cellar. They had barely gotten to it before hands seized them. Struggling,

Dana kicked and screamed, trying to get free. Every move she made resulted in tighter grips onto her arms and legs.

Shrieking, she and Minny were dragged outside amidst the yells of the mob. Dana gasped as they dumped her on the ground next to Sampson, who had been tied. Minny ran to her husband, but others snatched her and tied her as well.

Unable to stop the madness, Dana hunkered on her hands and knees, watching as people looted the house. Delicate items crashed and smashed on the floor, sending shards everywhere. She listened as they stomped around the house and stampeded up the stairs. More banging and crashing ensued. Dana glanced up at Kenny, who watched the proceedings with Bert by his side. He refused to meet her gaze.

Hatred filled Dana as people ran out of the house, carrying valuables that did not belong to them. She couldn't understand how things came to this in such a short period of time. Clanging and banging filled the air as people tossed items into the vehicle they had brought.

"To the fields," shouted Bert.

Instantly, the mob ran off into the massive fields that Sampson had just planted. They yelled and screamed in their riotous state. Dana listened to their pounding feet as they took off.

Kenny finally glanced at her with a dispassionate look. He broke it immediately as Dana continued to glare at him. Within minutes, the lights of fires sprang up, covering the fields. She knew where the flames had originated, the underground orchards and grooves. The sound of the melee filled her ears. Despite the distance, they sounded as though they were right next door.

While those guarding them had their backs turned, Dana undid Minny's wrists. Her fingers tugged at the taut rope, pulling it loose bit by bit. Relief filled her when it finally came undone.

Freed, Minny quickly unhooked Sampson's ties, freeing both his ankles and wrists. Without waiting for the blood to flow back into his limbs, Sampson charged one of those next to them. He threw the man to the ground, wrenching his weapon from him. Swiftly, Sampson smacked the other with it.

He handed Dana a key. "Take the truck and get out of here."

Dana looked at the key, not wanting to leave him alone. "What about you?"

"Don't worry about me."

Dana started to go before whirling around. "Karl!" she said. "He's too old to be able to handle them. What if they go to his place?"

"You and Minny go find Karl. Get him and bring him back here. We'll meet by the barn, or what's left of it once these idiots are through."

"What are you going to do?" asked Minny, concerned.

"Save what I can of my property," said Sampson.

"Be careful," Minny kissed her husband.

"You too."

They separated. Sampson ran into the field after the mob while Minny and Dana jumped into his truck.

The engine started immediately. Dana shoved it into gear and drove off down the dirt road to the town. She sped onward, not caring if the truck bounced and jostled them about. Smoke filled the sky from burning fires. Dana hoped that they made it to Karl's in time, knowing that a man in his 70s would be ill-suited to defend himself against a mob.

A throng of people blocked the road into town. Quickly, Dana swerved to the left, hanging on tightly to the wheel as the back wheels left the ground before crashing back into it. Dust and rock flew everywhere as she turned and swerved to avoid hitting the people, but not wanting to stop. Another swerve to the right and Dana crashed through an abandoned building as she charged into town. Rioters darted about with Molotov cocktails and bandanas wrapped around their faces to prevent themselves from being identified.

One man dashed in front of her. Swiftly, Dana jerked the wheel, bringing the truck to a halt as she barely missed the man. He banged his fists on the side of the vehicle, shouting curses and insults. Dana shifted into first and took off.

With little concern for anyone else who might run in front of her, she slammed the accelerator and charged uphill to Karl's place. Smoke made seeing difficult. Both Dana and Minny coughed as it seeped in through the vents.

Another crowd of rioters headed her way. Without hesitating, Dana did a 180 and plowed down a back road before turning back to Karl's. Homemade explosive devices thundered around her as enraged men and women chucked them. Others ran around with their arms full of items that they had stolen.

Dana noticed that Betsy's diner crumbled under the weight of the roaring flames that consumed it. She hoped the woman hadn't been in there when it happened. People hauled out one of her stoves, carrying it down the road. Soon, they tossed it through a window of another business.

The words "death to greed" were spray-painted on the sides of other buildings.

"Go this way," said Minny pointing to the left.

Dana turned the truck. She dodged and swerved to avoid accidents as she followed Minny's directions to Karl's. Within 10 minutes, they had navigated their way through the streets. Dana slammed the brakes, coming to a screeching halt as she stopped in front of Karl's house. The other houses around him were engulfed in flames.

Knowing there wasn't much time, Dana burst out of the truck and raced up the walk to the front door. She pushed it open, not bothering to knock.

"Karl!"

No answer.

Dana looked around the messy house. "Karl!"

She ran from room to room. No sign of him. Even his work room was empty.

"Karl!"

Panic filled Dana as Karl continued to not answer. She hoped she wasn't too late. The sounds of the mob drew closer.

"KARL!"

"Here!"

Dana ran upstairs to his bedroom. "Karl, come on, we need to leave."

"I know. I know. But I got to find it."

"Find what?" demanded Dana.

"It's here somewhere," said Karl as he rummaged around his room in vain.

"What are you looking for?"

"My wife's journal. She kept one before she died."

Shouts drew nearer. The building next door lit fire as people flung torches on it.

"Karl, we don't have time."

Dana snatched Karl's arm and yanked him out of the room. "No! Let me go!"

She refused his pleas. A window smashed as flaming rocks were hurled through it. Instantly, the place went up in flames with all of the scattered papers and books.

"There it is!"

Karl broke free of Dana and ran into the upstairs study. She chased after him. Just as she reached the man, he grabbed a small leather-bound book, clutching it tightly as though it were the most precious thing on earth.

The incessant honking of a horn fueled Dana's movements. She seized Karl and threw him out of the study. Not wanting any more distractions, she clutched tightly to his arm as she dragged him down the stairs. Thick, black smoke filled the house as the fires spread. Coughing and choking, Dana managed to get Karl to the bottom of the stairs. Flames blocked the front door.

"Which way?" shouted Dana.

"This way."

Karl darted through the kitchen. Dana followed. He stopped at a white pantry door. Carefully, Karl opened it, making certain that nothing lay behind. Dana peered into the dark interior.

"This is a closet," she said.

"In!" Karl thrust her inside. Dana had expected to meet a wall, but instead, nothing was there to stop her. Karl shut the door behind them. He reached around her and pulled on a metal cord, flipping on a light.

"Follow me,"

Karl walked ahead of Dana, leading her through a small tunnel and down some stairs. When they reached the bottom, he jerked to the left.

"Help me with this," he said.

Dana studied the metal door that blocked their way. Realizing that this was a basement of sorts, she figured that Karl must have built this in case he ever needed to make a fast getaway. She reached for the metal door while Karl pushed from the other side. Together, they popped the door out of its holding, moving it to the side. Air struck them as it rushed in.

Karl motioned for Dana to go through. She did with him close behind. Together, they ran through the opening and climbed a ladder coming out somewhere in his yard.

The chaotic noise of the mob alerted Dana to their presence. She hauled Karl out of the hole. Hanging onto him, Dana ran as fast as she could without losing the old man. They charged for the street.

Dana halted when she reached the road. *Where was the truck?* Looking all around, she searched for Sampson's truck, but found no sign of it. A blaring horn caught her attention. The roaring of an engine drew closer as the truck pulled up and screeched to a stop.

"Get in," said Minny.

Dana opened the door and shoved Karl inside. She jumped in the truck bed, pounding on the window for Minny to go. They sped off. Expertly, Minny wormed her way through the mob and away from Karl's house, which now burned brightly. Some of the rioters pelted the truck with rocks. Dana covered her head as a few pebbles stung her skin.

The truck turned and careened down a hill before leveling out. Cold air brushed the top of Dana's head, causing her to shiver slightly. Hanging on tightly, she tried to ignore the cold as she watched the rioters destroy everything they found.

Graffiti dotted what used to be nice looking real estate. "Give us what we're owed," said one. On another building, the words "we have rights too" stood out in vivid green paint.

Anger filled Dana. She thought she had left all that behind and found a place where she could live as she chose. Now all that had been ripped away by a man who was so shortsighted, he never thought beyond his own needs.

As they hit one of the main roads heading out of town, Dana noticed the stables for the first time that night. Its doors hung on their hinges as holes dotted one of the walls. Debris lay everywhere.

"Poboy!" Dana jumped out of the truck, thinking only of her horse, her friend.

Minny slammed the brakes. "Dana!"

Dana ignored Minny's shouts, her thoughts rested only with Poboy. She ran through the mangled road and the junk that now filled it. Desperate to reach her horse, Dana shoved her way through a crowd. She pushed and prodded people, forcing them out of her way. Few paid her any heed. Thinking she was one of them, one man handed her a Molotov cocktail. Dana chucked it at another mob that approached. Quickly, she heaved her way past everyone until she burst through the other side.

Freed from the mass of people, Dana sprinted for the stables. Mr. Callors was nowhere to be found, but Dana didn't care. *Poboy*. She smacked into one of the hanging doors as she ran into the stables. Hay lay everywhere, mixed with feed that had been dumped. Manure lined the walls, as some thought it funny to chuck it at them.

Dana ran for Poboy's stall. Tears streamed down her cheeks when she reached it. Inside laid the young horse in a pool of blood. Someone had slashed its throat with a knife and wrote the words "wealth and greed killed the whores" on the wall behind him. Slowly, Dana entered Poboy's stall. She knelt down, reaching out with a shaking hand to touch him. All sounds from the riots faded. Only her horse's demise mattered to her.

The still soft fur of Poboy stunned Dana as she stroked him. She sat beside him, putting his head in her lap and ignoring the blood that dripped onto her pants. Carefully, Dana petted her friend. She knew he was dead, but she didn't want to accept it.

"I'm here, boy," she whispered. "I'm here."

Poboy's vacant eyes stared back at her. Gently, Dana brushed her hand over them, closing them. "You're just sleeping. Only sleeping."

Common sense told her this was a waste of time, but Dana's grief refused to release her. Poboy was her horse. She bought him, cared for him, and visited him each day. He had become her friend. Now he lay dead, killed by a bunch of thugs who thought the world owed them what they coveted. Poboy was innocent, yet he paid the ultimate price.

Crying, Dana refused to leave. She never heard the steps that approached her.

"I'm sorry," said Kenny as he looked at Dana cradling Poboy.

Sniffling, Dana looked into Kenny's eyes. "No you're not. You don't know the meaning of the word."

"Dana, I never expected this to happen."

"Well, what did you expect as you worked people up into a fit of anger?" Dana continued stroking Poboy's mane as though the horse might come back to life.

"I just wanted everyone to be equal."

Dana laughed. "You don't even know what that means."

More footsteps approached. Minny and Karl walked in, searching for Dana. They saw Dana cradling Poboy and knew not to rush her. Minny's eyes turned to Kenny, focusing on him with a venomous stare.

"What are you doing here?" she demanded.

"I just wanted to apologize," said Kenny.

Minny picked up a nearby shovel. "Boy, you got five seconds to get out of here before I beat you into your grave with this shovel."

Kenny glanced at Dana. "Dana…"

"Leave me alone," hissed Dana.

Despite the sorrow that filled Kenny's eyes, Dana only felt hatred toward him. He turned and left.

"Dana, we need to go." Karl lifted Dana by the arm.

"I can't leave him," said Dana.

"We need to leave. There's nothing you can do for him now." Delicately, Karl hauled Dana to her feet, forcing her to leave the stable. Minny followed close behind with the shovel in her hands, wary of anyone else that might chance upon them.

They reached the parked truck, which had remained untouched. Gently, Karl put Dana into the cab and sat beside her. Minny dumped the shovel in the back and got in the driver's seat. She rammed it into gear and pulled away.

Ignoring the mob, Minny steered the truck onto the dirt road and back to what remained of her home.

Dana remained silent the entire way. She stared blankly out the window, her eyes had gone dry. "Why Poboy?" she kept asking herself. She had never expected to love a horse so much, but her now broken heart just wanted to be left alone. Neither Karl, nor Minny spoke to her. They both knew that words meant nothing right then.

Minny paused when they reached the house. Only scorched remains were left. A few smoldering embers glowed, but the house was gone. "Forty years I've lived in this place," said Minny, "Sampson and I rebuilt the house many times after storms and floods, only to have it ripped away by a bunch of animals."

"My wife and I lived in my house for 50 years. We were married in that place," said Karl.

"I'm sorry," said Minny.

"What happened to her?" asked Dana, finally breaking her silence.

"One day, she said she didn't feel well. The next day, I buried her."

Dana looked into Karl's eyes. She saw the pain that was still there, even after the years that had passed since. "I'm sorry."

"No worries," said Karl. "I've had time to get over it."

"Does the pain ever stop?" asked Dana.

"In time, honey," said Minny. "In time."

Minny put her foot on the accelerator and headed for the barn. Sampson stood outside waiting for them.

"Those fools destroyed everything," said Sampson. "Apples and oranges are lying all over the place. They even chopped down the trees. And as though that weren't enough, they destroyed the climate controls and set them all on fire."

"Isn't much left of the house either," said Minny.

"I want you three to search through what's left of the house and this barn and salvage what you can. Only what we need though," said Sampson, "I'm going to go back to the fields and save what I can. Hopefully, I can gather enough to last us for the trip."

"Trip?" asked Karl.

"I'm not staying here," said Sampson. "If those idiots want my land, then they can have it and the mess they've made of it."

"Where will we go?" asked Minny.

Sampson put his hat back on. "I don't know."

He and Minny switched places, while Dana and Karl hopped out of the truck. Within seconds, Sampson had gone to salvage what was left of his life's work.

Minny's hands wrapped around Dana's shoulders. "Come on," she said, gently. "There isn't much time and we have a lot to do."

Dana plopped the last bag into the back of the truck. The others waited for her in the cab. Though a tight fit, they managed to squeeze four people in there.

Kenny had followed Dana to the farm, hoping to convince her to stay.

"I have nothing to say to you," said Dana before he could speak.

"Dana, I never meant for any of this to happen. But sometimes, bad things happen for the better."

Dana glared at Kenny. "What do you want?"

"I've come to ask you to stay."

Dana laughed.

"Dana, please. I do care about you. I want you to stay here. Together, we can lead this place to a better life. We can…"

"No."

"What?"

"No," said Dana. "I'm not staying. I don't care what you want, Kenny. I no longer care about what you're thinking. You wanted to turn things upside down for your own ends and you succeeded. I hope you are happy with what you've achieved."

Dana got into the truck.

"Dana, please…"

She slammed the door as Sampson started the engine. "This is your new world, Kenny. You live in it."

Wheels crunched on the gravel as the truck sped off in the morning sunlight, leaving Kenny alone with his accomplishments.

CHAPTER

TWENTY-ONE

Colonel Fernau hunched over the holographic monitor in his office. A satisfied smile crept across his face as he watched the image on the screen. Glad that he had ordered the drones sent into the wasteland, he now had something he could use to track his most hated enemy.

Colonel Fernau enlarged the image so that he could see the face. Dana's saddened eyes stared back at him, unaware she was being watched.

"I've got you now, Miss Ginary," whispered Colonel Fernau to himself. "You will not escape me this time."

Get the entire Dystopia Trilogy

Dystopia (Book 1)
Tempered Steel (Book 2)
Liberty's Torch (Book 3)

**Imagine living in a world where
everything you do is controlled.**

Dana Ginary lives in a world where every aspect of her
life is controlled by the Dystopian Government. Forced to
work in Waste Management, her life becomes a nightmare
with hunger and survival is her only constant. Before she
knows it, she is caught up in a resistance movement and
exiled from Dystopia, forced to find her way in the barren wastelands. While there, she must learn to live independently and discover how far she is willing to go to live
and achieve freedom.

Also available on audio.

About the Author

Janet McNulty began her writing career with the Legends Lost series, published under the name of Nova Rose.

Ms. McNulty began the Dystopia Trilogy over a year ago with an idea she had carried with her since high school. A fan of books such as *Animal Farm, 1984, and Brave New World*, she decided to create her own vision of a world gone terribly wrong.

More by Janet McNulty

The Mellow Summers Series

Sugar And Spice And Not So Nice
Frogs, Snails, And A Lot Of Wails
An Apple A Day Keeps Murder Away
Three Little Ghosts
Oh Holy Ghost
Where Trouble Roams
Two Ghosts Haunt A Grove
Trick Or Treat Or Murder
Roses Are Red…He's Dead
Double, Double Nothing But Trouble
Ring Around The Rosy, Not Another Ghosty

Mellow Summers moves to Vermont to attend college, accompanied by her friend Jackie. They soon find themselves running into ghosts and one mystery after another.

The Solaris Saga

Each novel has a companion coloring book.

Solaris Seethes
Solaris Seeks
Solaris Strays
Solaris Soars

Every myth has a beginning

After escaping the destruction of her home planet, Lanyr, with the help of the mysterious Solaris, Rynah must put her faith in an ancient legend. Never one to believe in stories and legends, she is forced to follow the ancient tales of her people: tales that also seem to predict her current situation.

Forced to unite with four unlikely heroes from an unknown planet (the philosopher, the warrior, the lover, the inventor) in order to save the Lanyran people, Rynah and Solaris embark on an adventure that will shatter everything Rynah once believed.

Also available on audio.

The Legends Lost Series

Published under Nova Rose

Tesnayr
Amborese
Galdin

Enter the Lands of Tesnayr and join on an epic fantasy adventure that spans over 1,500 years.

Begin with Tesnayr, the first king of the five lands as he unites the against a savage foe bent on their destruction.

Next, Join Amborese as she fights reclaim the throne after her family was forced to flee from it.

Thinking peace has finally entered the land, follow Galdin as he returns to Tesnayr to find it greatly hanged. Barbarians, led by a mysterious sorcerer, burn and destroy as they go. And only Galdin can stop them if he chooses to accept his fate.

Grandpa's Stories

My grandfather grew up in Arizona during the 1920s and 1930s. One week after the attack on Pearl Harbor he joined the Navy. During the summer of 2012, my mother visited him and recorded his stories about growing up, World War II, and his time as an employee at the Pacific Bell Telephone Company. This is the history of the 20th century as he lived it. These recordings make up this book. These are his words.

Something for the Little Ones

The Dragon Who series

The Dragon Who was Afraid of the Dark
The Dragon Who Went to the Moon
The Dragon Who Found a Monster Party
The Dragon Who Found a Spider in His Shoe
The Dragon Who Explored the Sea
The Dragon Who Caught a Cold

The Fairy Who series

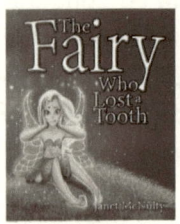

The Fairy Who Lost a Tooth
The Fairy Who Got Lost

The Mr. Chili series

Mr. Chili's Chili
Mr. Chili Goes To School
Mr. Chili's Halloween
Mr. Chili's Christmas

Others:

Mrs. Duck and the Dragon
The Hungry Washing Machine
Rhymes-a-lot
Are You the Monster Under My Bed?
How Do You Catch An Alien